What Does Your Writing Reveal?

W

Tall and angular wings expose the natural leader—a take-charge personality who can get things done.

D

A pointy belly indicates a no-nonsense attitude. This is someone who deals with life on his own terms and is persistent when pursuing goals.

Y

Upright with outstretched arms shows a champagne spirit—an optimist with unqualified gratitude for each new day.

V

A wide mouth discloses a potent sex-drive and an enthusiasm for bedroom experimentation.

R

Long legs reveal a cautious nature—one who is steady but perhaps slow to commit.

Instant Insight

Secrets of Life, Love, and Destiny Revealed in Your Handwriting

CASH PETERS

WARNER BOOKS

A Time Warner Company

Warner Books, Inc., 1271 Avenue of the Americas, New York, NY 10020
Visit our Web site at http://warnerbooks.com

W A Time Warner Company

Printed in the United States of America
First Printing: June 1998
10 9 8 7 6 5 4 3 2 1

Library of Congress Cataloging-in-Publication Data

Peters, Cash.
    Instant insight : secrets of life, love, and destiny revealed in
your handwriting / Cash Peters.
        p.   cm.
    ISBN: 0-446-67355-2
    1. Graphology.   I. Title.
BF891.P48   1998
155.2'82—dc21   97-29937
                                                       CIP

Book design by H. Roberts Design
Cover design by Jon Valk

ATTENTION: SCHOOLS AND CORPORATIONS
WARNER books are available at quantity
discounts with bulk purchase for educational,
business, or sales promotional use. For
information, please write to: SPECIAL SALES
DEPARTMENT, WARNER BOOKS, 1271 AVENUE
OF THE AMERICAS, NEW YORK, NY 10020

Acknowledgments

This book could not have been completed without the generous help and advice of several key people:

Tim Moat at Headline Communications, Peter Clapperton, Ian Hardy and Bruce Hyman. Also, autograph collectors Walter Burks and Richard Davie for putting their respective private collections at my disposal. I owe a particular debt of thanks to Debra Goldstein, my agent at the William Morris Agency, whose encouragement and unerring faith carried this project forward and made all the difference. Her assistants Jessica and Maia deserve a mention too, I'm sure, for dealing so graciously with the endless to-ing and fro-ing.

One can only admire the courage of the editorial staff at Warner Books for seeing the potential in this book at the start, and the gentle tenacity and enthusiasm of my editor, Diana Baroni, who helped bring it home in the end.

Finally, an extraspecial thank-you to Loveday Miller, Mandy Wheeler and Gary Robertson for their unerring advice and support, but most of all, I guess, to my dad and my brother Andrew for standing by me and showing such generosity and love under great personal pressure.

—C.P.

Contents

✍ Introduction / ix

✍ First Steps / 1

✍ How to Approach a Piece of Handwriting / 9

✍ Alphabet: a–z / 11

✍ Alphabet: A–Z / 111

✍ Troubleshooting Guide / 208

Introduction

*t*his book is about handwriting: yours, mine, your lover's, your lawyer's, your best friend's—even Madonna's writing, I'm sure, is in these pages somewhere. But it's not just about handwriting; it's also about love, happiness, fulfillment, freedom, success—all the things we really care about.

In short, this is a book about Life.

Up to now, when you were writing letters, Christmas cards, thank-you notes or grocery lists, I bet you never once gave a thought to the hidden messages concealed behind the words. You just scribbled the things you wanted to say and then forgot about it, like we all do. What you perhaps don't realize is that every single time you put pen to paper, you reveal the most amazing truths about yourself—your character, your personal experience, your childhood, your hopes and dreams, in fact your whole life story, past, present and future. Handwriting tells us the kind of person you are, not just on the outside—your personality and all that stuff other folks see—but the *real* you buried deep inside.

On one level, it works a bit like a Polaroid camera, taking an instant snapshot of your life as it stands right this second. Are you happy or sad, fulfilled by your work or frustrated, buzzing with good health or feeling gloomy and under the weather?

Whatever mood you're in, whatever you are thinking and feeling now, this moment, will affect the shape of the words as you draw them on the page. Which probably explains why your handwriting seems to change so often.

Have you noticed how, on days when you're in a positive frame of mind and doing just fine, it tends to be bouncy, confident and readable, while on other days, when things aren't going so well, it looks hopelessly random and chaotic, as though your words were written during a severe earth tremor? Well, that's because handwriting is a direct product of your subconscious mind. Whatever you're really thinking and feeling on the inside spills out onto the page—you can't help yourself. Later on, as circumstances shift and your mood lightens, and as you begin to feel different in some way about yourself and your situation, then your handwriting automatically changes to reflect that. It's very clever.

Then again, you could also think of your handwriting as a mirror, reflecting back at you—sometimes with devastating accuracy—the *kind* of person you've become over the years. Few of us ever get the chance to see ourselves the way others see us, and I'm pretty sure we'd have a shock if we did; but as soon as you start writing, out it all comes: your temperament, your behavior, all those special qualities, good and not so good, that make you the unique individual you are. Your handwriting can also be used to measure your level of self-esteem, how fulfilled you are by your work, whether you are generous and loving in your relationships or mean and self-centered; your handwriting can even, believe it or not, reveal your views on sex and how experienced you are between the sheets. Yes, it's that specific!

More importantly, though, the way you shape your words shows clearly how close you are to living out your destiny, the life you were born to lead: whether you are still searching for answers to the many riddles in your world or have discovered what your

Divine purpose is while you're here on the planet. That is the kind of information we all need to know, and that, I believe, is what this book will help you to find out—not just for yourself, but for others too.

All you need to make it work is a note or card written by someone you would like to understand a little better (I guess you might include yourself in this too!), then simply flick through the Alphabet Pages to find the letter-shapes that correspond most closely to the ones you find in the handwriting, and read off what each one means. It really is as easy as that. There is nothing to learn and no difficult explanations to understand. In every case, you should be able to gain valuable insights into the way other people think and why they behave as they do.

If you have never studied this subject before, I guarantee you will be amazed at the amount of personal and private information built into all those tiny loops and squiggles, crosses and twirls you call your handwriting. By exploring the meaning behind each letter of the alphabet, you will be able to unlock the secrets of just about everyone you know, even if they don't write in English. Provided their language is based on the standard A-through-Z alphabet, the principles in this book should work for them and explain their personality. Every piece of scribble will suddenly come alive with fresh meaning. Never again, I promise you, will you look at a postcard or a love letter, a handwritten menu in a restaurant, or your own grocery list pinned to the refrigerator without seeing the true significance behind the words.

First Steps

Most people know something about handwriting. They don't think they do, and they certainly wouldn't claim to be graphologists (the fancy name given to anyone who has studied this subject in great detail over many years); even so, they know what it's like to pick up a "vibe" from a piece of writing, usually based on what it looks like and the way the words are laid out across the page. I'm sure you must have had this experience.

For instance, let's suppose you came across handwriting that was large and vibrant, like this:

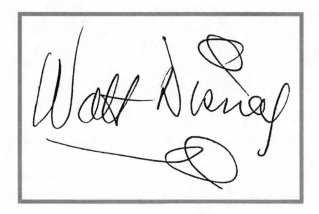

What conclusions would you draw? That the person who
wrote it was lively and enthusiastic and probably quite a character? Sure you would. Everything about it screams "Hey, gather
'round, I've got this great new idea!" It makes perfect sense that
the positive energy a guy like Walt Disney channeled into his
everyday activities—such as walking, eating and talking—would
be the same energy he'd put into his handwriting.

Similarly, if you received a letter in the mail and every line of
it was tiny and cramped, something like this:

> Menlo Park N.J. Feby 12 1877.
>
> Dear Sir
>
> Your communication of the 10th
> asking my opinion as to the reasonableness of a certain change of
> $249. forming part of a bill presented to your company by L.W.
> Serrell for services rendered is received.
>
> Very Respy
> Thos. A. Edison

You would most likely think, hmm, now, anyone who writes *that*
small must have a pretty low-key personality. And even if you

didn't actually think that, it's still the kind of impression that such tiny, cramped handwriting would leave on your mind. There's nothing flamboyant about it. A quick glance at its precise, controlled style tells you that the great Thomas Edison was everything you'd expect him to be: conscientious, reliable, scientific, unrelenting in his approach, someone who kept on working at a project until he got it right.

I give many talks and seminars on this subject each year, and I'm always amazed how many members of the audience have already worked out a few of the basic principles for themselves, not because they're interested in handwriting particularly, but because they're observant people who like to show an interest in the way their fellow humans operate. So they tend to know, for example, what it means when writing has a natural slope to it. If the words gradually dip downward across the page—I'm thinking of something like this:

Then they figure the person who wrote it must have a "down" outlook on life and be in a generally pessimistic frame of mind. And they'd be right. See how tired and lifeless it looks, almost as if there is a large lead weight attached to the end of each line, dragging the words toward the floor. Clearly, whatever is eating at this guy, it's really sapping his spirit. As he sees it, things are bound to get worse before they get better, and, of course, so long as he clings on to this belief, that's precisely what will happen.

Whereas when the handwriting rises gently:

> *[handwritten text in box]* Such a good time but probably spent far too much time in the Casino —last

You can be sure you're dealing with someone who believes everything will turn out fine in the end. Just look at that upswing! So buoyant, so packed with joyful optimism. Even when things go wrong, this person won't allow himself to stay defeated or downcast for very long. There are always better times around the next corner, always good things ahead. In each case, you can conclude that the greater the degree of slope, upward or downward, the more pronounced the trait will be.

One other feature that my students often work out for themselves is the slant of the writing, whether it is angled to the right or the left. They've discovered that a right slant:

> *[handwritten text in box]* thanks a lot, the present was lovely,

usually belongs to a more dynamic kind of individual, someone who lives in the moment, takes direct action, and makes things happen for himself, rather than indulging in a whole load of unnecessary anxiety beforehand. This type of person might not admit to being "dynamic" exactly, and maybe he's not—not in any conventional way at least—but there is still an energy there, a drive and determination that will help him push his plans through to fruition. This "direct action" kind of energy becomes even more obvious when you compare it to writing that slants to the left:

> I really have a lot to do before going on a trip. Travelling can be very trying but it should be great fun.

This person is the opposite. Whenever he can, he holds back and moves at his own comfortable pace. Somehow, that's the kind of feeling you get from it too. When he takes action—and it may be sooner, it may be later—but when he does, he needs to know exactly what is expected of him *before* he gets started. Someone like this may be just as dynamic as the forward-slant type, but when the heat is on there is always a voice at the back of his mind urging him to take everything a step at a time and build solid foundations under his plans. I hardly need to add that handwriting that stands upright without any slant at all usually balances the two extremes, a case of "never commit too quickly, never hesitate for too long."

Many other handwriting principles have the same kind of logic to them as these and are therefore just as easy to grasp. It makes sense, for instance, that the person who is impatient and sharp-tongued and has what you might call a "spiky" character will have impatient, sharp, spiky writing, just as you might expect someone who is soft, tender and innocent to have soft, rounded, innocent writing. It's simple. Mostly it comes down to common sense and observation.

One last point worth mentioning: margins.

> If ever you come across this kind of situation, where the left-hand margin is very large and spacious, it means the writer is extremely cautious. He's going to think long and hard before committing to anything and won't ever be dragged into making hasty decisions. The slimmer the left-hand margin, the less cautious the person is likely to be.

Whereas an oversized right-hand margin, like the one here, where each line of writing stops short of the edge of the paper, indicates caution of a different kind. This person is reliable. *Very* reliable. He's so reliable, in fact, that he'll always be on time for everything, won't overrun deadlines if he can help it, and will always get work finished ahead of time wherever possible. If you see a tiny or nonexistent right-hand margin, don't expect the writer to be particularly reliable or strict on deadlines. Some tasks will get done on time, some won't. Accept it. That's just how he is.

Margins vary greatly from person to person, so it's difficult to generalize. I do know that someone who fills every inch of the paper top to bottom, left to right, until it begins to look like a wall coated in graffiti, is likely to have problems bringing his emotional responses under control. Often, this is a cry for attention from a neglected soul desperate to be heard and accepted. So many needs are going unmet, there's so much to be said, with never enough time or opportunity to say it.

In life, he may appear impetuous and intense, and may tend to be fairly self-absorbed, a good deal more interested in his own world than yours.

On the other hand, if there are huge margins all the way around, then you're probably dealing with someone who has a very specific angle on life. This type of writer believes he's got all the elements in his world figured out. He knows his place and craves regularity, which means he is probably missing out on all kinds of opportunities that would expand his horizons in so many new and interesting ways. Too much control, too much structure; too much effort goes into living up to other people's expectations and not enough into having fun or being naturally spontaneous.

That's really all you need to know to get started.

The rest of the book is arranged in the form of a directory. The small letters, a through z, come first, and then the capitals, A through Z.

These pages contain hundreds of insights and discoveries drawn from years rich in experience. I sincerely hope that, whatever answers you may be searching for in your life right now, you find something here to help and guide you, or at least to point you toward a brighter, more fulfilling future.

—C.P.

How to Approach
a Piece of Handwriting

1. The best way to begin your analysis is letter by letter. So if the first two words are "Dear Barbara," for example, you should turn to the *D* page in the directory and search for the variation of the *D* that looks most like the one in the handwriting, and read off the meaning. Then do the same with *e* and *a* and *r*, and as many other letters as necessary until you have built up an overall portrait of the writer. If you can't find the variation you're looking for, please don't give up. Either choose the closest match and adapt the definition or, better still, overlook the letter altogether for the time being. Not being able to find the occasional *S* or *p* shouldn't stop you from exploring someone's personality in significant detail. Don't be afraid to combine different letter explanations if that's what it takes to get a more accurate picture.

2. Try to avoid taking single letters in isolation. This is important. Otherwise you could end up with misleading information. Human beings are complex creatures, each one boasting many unique facets to his or her character. The explanation offered by one letter may have its meaning completely changed by another. So analyze as many different letters as you can until you get the broadest picture possible.

3. There may be several variations on a single letter shape within the same piece of handwriting. Don't be alarmed. This doesn't mean the writer is crazy or dysfunctional; it simply reflects the many subtle shades of his character. Treat each variation as one more precious fragment of his personality—it's not the whole story, just a small part of it.

4. You will find alongside each letter variation a brief descriptive phrase, often no more than a word or two. This identifies the specific characteristic of the letter's shape, the one that gives it its distinctive quality. This will help you if you find a letter in the handwriting that is a combination of two different shapes.

5. As you will see, throughout the book I refer to "the writer" as a he. This is for the usual reason of convenience. To have done otherwise would have caused more problems than it solved. Rest assured, though, that all the principles, definitions and explanations given here apply equally to women as they do to men.

Alphabet a–z

a

Sensitivity

Many people spend their entire life taking the easy way out, the soft option. Faced with adversity or criticism or awkward confrontations, their first impulse is to flee. And who can blame them? Understandably, they want to dodge any experience that might give rise to feelings of fear, rejection, embarrassment or any one of a dozen other painful and destructive emotions. However, this pleasure-over-pain philosophy overlooks one simple fact of life: It was never meant to be easy.

Life is not a cozy ride for the faint-hearted. It's a free-flowing adventure, packed with incidents and experiences of all kinds—some joyous and pleasurable, others so tough and challenging that it takes almost all our reserves of ingenuity and resilience to overcome them. Right there, though, in times of great adversity, is when we discover what we're really made of. Not when everything in the garden is rosy and things are just bowling along merrily without a hitch, but when our back is right up against the wall and circumstances force us to come out fighting.

The moment we accept this, the moment we are prepared to desensitize ourselves and, rather than cowering before our fears, rise up to meet them, is when setbacks, obstacles and confrontations become stepping-stones to our greater good, helping us to become just that little bit stronger, wiser and more resilient, so that when future crises strike we are better equipped to handle them in a more positive and constructive way.

Generally it is our failures that civilize us.
Triumph confirms us in our habits.
—Clive James

---

a

✎ **Check out** the size and roundness of the *a*. Generally, the fuller and rounder it is, the more sensitive the writer is going to be. If the *a* is small and tight, then he is less vulnerable to being hurt by criticism or adversity.

Tight, with tail: Quite a strong character, the sort to speak his mind and tell it like it is. Knows what he wants and is not easily thrown off course. Understands his rights and likes to exert them. Guards and protects his sensitive side. Many lessons have been learned over the years. Nowadays, not easily outsmarted.

Gently rounded: Strikes a reasonable balance. Open and sensitive, sure, but not too much. Usually willing to listen to criticism; is only hurt by harsh words intended to wound. Deals with problems in a practical way. Has enough reserves of strength and knowledge to keep him level-headed. Calm, approachable, but firm.

Big, puffed up: Far too sensitive and probably defensive too. He's either quite shy at heart or he's compensating for emotional weaknesses and a deep fear of getting hurt by being difficult or, in some cases, aggressive toward others (attack being the best form of defense, etc.). Needs to explore and confront long-term insecurities.

Shielded: Outer shell indicates a certain toughness. Unwilling to appear vulnerable. Fears exploitation. Old wounds still hurt; harsh lessons have been learned. Has constructed a shield around himself as added protection against outside attack. Underneath: an old pussycat.

Droopy: Overshadowed by personal problems. Experiencing a temporary lack of joy. Emotional dark clouds undermine confidence in the future. Things may not be as bad as they seem, though. Needs to look for the good in the situation and wait for an upswing in affairs.

Rounded, with tail: Kind at heart, but with attitude. Has firm opinions, but is generally happy to discuss points and listen to others. Willing to assert himself where necessary and exert rights for the benefit of all. An interesting mix of mild and strong, knowing and innocent.

Small, delicate: Easily hurt. Can't overlook insults or criticism. Takes personal comments to heart and chews over their meaning. May seem as though he's just _waiting_ to be offended sometimes. Needs to lighten up and be more assertive.

Looped: Has many reservations about life, so can't relax. Each step seems filled with dangers. Tries to be brave and take positive action, but secretly fears making mistakes. Needs to worry less, have more faith, believe that things always work out fine in the end if only we'll let them.

Poised: Has confidence in ideas and plans and is unafraid of presenting them to others. Enjoys free discussion and likes to receive feedback. Not scared of criticism—it's all part of the game. Addresses issues head-on. Positive approach usually wins positive results.

Tall, upright: Slow to commit. Afraid of consequences of actions. Hates giving in to whims or temptation. May criticize people for being impulsive and acting without thought for others while secretly wishing he could do the same. It's time to let go of fears.

Crushed: Has been beaten back by life and is forced to survive on wits. Stands his ground; can seem tough and immovable. Won't let others trample over him. May appear defensive and even insensitive at times, but is just protecting his feelings and territory.

A thank-you from **Diana, Princess of Wales.** *Such a sensitive, open hand. See the way her a's are so very open and rounded? This shows how hurt she could be by harsh criticism as well as the behavior of other people. A caring, supportive woman, keener than most to be loved and appreciated.*

b

financial security

It is a mistake to assume that everybody perceives money in exactly the same way. For some, ten million dollars in the bank, closets full of designer clothes, sprawling homes in New York and L.A. with a private jet to fly them between the two are the very essentials of life. Anything less would seem like total failure.

Then there are those with simpler values. They won't allow themselves to become mesmerized by the illusion of glamour and power that accompanies wealth. Even if they do accumulate plenty of money, they still see it for what it is—a flow of energy, a reward for believing in themselves and daring to strive for their goals and a passport to greater freedom. By their philosophy, riches are measured not in sacks of gold, fast cars or drawers packed with diamond jewelry, but in simple kindnesses, self-respect, peace of mind through an easy conscience and a readiness to give and receive love. These are the things that really matter.

If you are wealthy and happy, then you're rich. If you haven't got a nickel to your name but you're still happy, then you are rich too. Money only makes you wealthier, it can't buy you happiness. No amount of dollar bills will ever compensate for low self-esteem, poor health or a cold heart. The qualities we should all be striving for— such as joy, contentment and gratitude—begin on the inside; they're either right there in your heart or they're not. Which is why you must make a point of being happy now, today, with whatever you have and whomever you're with. Dream of having more by all means—we all need a bigger, brighter star to shoot for—but in the end, never lose sight of the things that really count.

Money is better than poverty,
if only for financial reasons.
—Woody Allen

---

b

Check out the height of the upright stem in proportion to the round bowl. The taller the stem, the more the writer dreams of material wealth. The larger and more complete the bowl, the greater the effort he will put into achieving those dreams. An incomplete bowl can often point to a shortage of money.

Plain, complete: A healthy attitude toward money. Earns it, saves it, spends it, respects it. Has an understanding of what he is worth and seeks proper reward for his talents. He figures financial security has to be worked for. Luckily, he's shrewd enough to make sure he gets whatever he desires.

Open: Always wants more. This person never seems to be satisfied. There is a deep and strong belief here that anything is possible, but constant striving for the best could lead to dissatisfaction. It may be that his income is never quite enough, or just that his expenses are too great. Either way, outside factors get in the way of progress.

Oversized: Knows what he wants and is determined that others should give it to him. May assert his own interests over those of others. Insecurity about what he's really worth means this writer tries that much harder to make a big impression on bosses and colleagues, especially if that leads to a bigger paycheck.

Bold with loop: Shrewd, assertive, direct. Keen not just to make money but to keep it, too. Always dreaming up plans to earn more. Also clever enough to put it somewhere beyond the reach of anyone who might want it back. A smart cookie. Knows what he deserves and is not too shy to ask for it.

Looped, open: On the lookout for extra money. Attitude toward cash is influenced strongly by childhood conditioning. Has a deep fear of losing what he has, so he strives harder to keep it and make more. Whatever he gets, though, it never seems quite enough.

Plunging down: May be grasping. Wants what others have got. Not afraid to stake his claim and then hang on to what he makes. Tactics may be subtle, but make no mistake, this person is out to win, ensuring that nobody else gets their hands on his loot.

Tall stem, tiny bowl: Dreams of making big bucks, but inside is afraid of poverty and ends up with less than he deserves. May not have laid down solid foundations before striving for financial goals. The solution: dream realistically, spend fearlessly and expect miracles always.

Up and over: Probably has enough money already, yet still he wants more. May be greedy or just plain insecure. Doesn't like to miss out on a good thing. Forever setting new goals and reaching out toward fresh horizons. Keeps trying, never lets up.

Incomplete: This usually points to cash-flow problems. There's more going out than coming in. This person may have difficulty making ends meet and, despite seeming happy about the situation, is probably quite worried underneath. Needs to put financial affairs on a firmer footing.

Pulled apart: What a struggle! The need to spend and the desire to save are slugging it out. The problem is, the writer is not in control—outside forces play havoc with his plans and his efforts to accumulate the amount of cash he'd like. Sometime soon he must put his foot down!

an open mind

Rigid opinions are saboteurs. They suffocate learning, stifle initiative and prevent us from understanding the bigger picture and where we, as individuals, fit into it. I remember seeing a sign outside a church once that said, "If you are not growing, then you are dying." It might have said, "If you are not learning, then you're stagnating."

Nothing is permanent, nothing stays exactly the same from one day, even from one second, to the next. Change is the only constant in life. So why fight it? Why not lower our defenses and embrace it? That means opening ourselves up to shifting trends and circumstances and if necessary reevaluating all those things we believe in—even the very core principles we have lived by for many years, if that's what it takes—in the light of new evidence that says "there is a better way." By refusing to bend, by remaining locked into all these outdated attitudes and belief patterns, insisting that *our* opinion, *our* set of principles, *our* chosen path is the "right" one, we stand in our own light, blocking our chances of becoming better, more productive human beings. In other words, we're not growing, but dying.

There should be no room in our lives for prejudice, bigotry or even, I would suggest, cynical attitudes. Cynicism, as a currency of thought, is worthless. It corrodes the spirit and wrecks our faith in human nature by denying everything that is beautiful, simple, honest and wholesome and concentrating exclusively on the negative: What is wrong, what is bad, who's on the make. The more we search for the basic good and decency in all people, regardless of their color, sexual orientation, religion or other markers, then the more good, decent people we will attract into our life and the more our trust will be rewarded.

All great truths begin as blasphemies.
—George Bernard Shaw

C

Average, round: Open-minded. Likes to know what is going on. Any information welcome. Wants to learn, needs to know, makes the effort to find out new and interesting facts. Accepts that others have a right to their own beliefs and lifestyles. Not the type to disapprove. "Live and let live" is the message here.

Flattened: Discerning. Only interested in matters that directly concern him. If it's not relevant it'll be tossed in the garbage, or just ignored. This person knows what he likes and won't want to get involved in peripheral issues. Sticks to the facts; doesn't waste time poking his nose into things that don't concern him.

Curling: Cynical, doubting, wise to any scheme or scam that's going on. Won't be fooled, blocks out the approaches of anyone who is on the make. Experience has taught a few tough lessons. Now more guarded than ever. Could miss out on potentially beneficial opportunities by being too suspicious. Needs to lighten up.

Looped: Uh-oh! Entrenched views, firm opinions, unshifting beliefs. This person has lived a lot and endured a few "bum steers" in the past, so these days he's determined not to fall for any of the old tricks. Some folk are not to be trusted, others are cheats and liars—that's what he believes, and he's sticking to it.

Looped behind: Finds reassurance in shared views. Justifies outlook and attitudes by reference to others: "Look, *they* do it, so it must be okay." Fear of standing out from the crowd leads to conformity for conformity's sake. Better to break free of the herd and dare to be different.

Outstretched: Eager for answers. Catches snippets of news like raindrops. Always wants to be ahead of the game: the first to know, the first to learn the truth, the first with the latest data. Any old detail will do, frankly. Just hates to think he's missing out or falling behind.

Upstretched: Has a very specific frame of interest, so keep to the point and make it quick. Says, "I can't be fascinated by *everything*, can I?" Too busy exploring his own little world to waste time venturing into yours. Don't try talking him around. If he tells you he's not interested, he isn't. Accept it.

Flattened: Tastes and opinions are probably fairly immature. Has never expanded his mind or ventured beyond teenage fascinations. Could behave selfishly, even heartlessly at times, and without considering consequences of words or actions. Not malicious, just naïve and unthinking.

Backbone: Very definite preconceptions about life. A rigid approach leads to a lack of flexibility in views and behavior. Possibly a cultural thing. He feels as though he is dragging a weight of experiences and conditioning behind him that he can never escape or shrug off.

Blocked by next letter: Often, this person can't see the forest for the trees. Feels overwhelmed by big tasks. Deals with one job at a time and won't allow himself to be sidetracked. So caught up in small details that he misses the bigger picture.

d

Showing anger

Human beings were made to go wild occasionally. When life is getting on top of us, when nothing's going right and we feel like shouting and screaming and cussing at the sky, then that's what we should do.

It's *okay* to drop the cool exterior once in a while and let off steam. Rage, frustration and grief may make other folk feel uncomfortable, but these negative emotions are just as natural to us as the positive ones such as joy, enthusiasm or excitement. We can't wish them away by suppressing or ignoring them. Well, we can try, but all we're really doing is trapping them inside in little emotional pockets, where they stew and fester until, like lava from an erupting volcano, they eventually force their way out by another route—often in the form of psychosomatic symptoms. Strange as it seems, being too nice can do your body a lot of harm.

Those angelic types, the people who strive to be so patient and long suffering, may earn themselves a reputation for being easygoing and for never losing their cool even in a crisis, but at what cost? By storing up a whole load of painful feelings, remaining passive and smiley, claiming everything in their world is "juss wunnerful" when really, inside, they're hurting like crazy and all they want to do is kick and scream and throw plates at the wall, they're placing a huge strain on their nervous systems.

Anger doesn't have to be a destructive force. These feelings can be vented in all kinds of *con*structive ways. You could pound them away with a game of basketball, or breathe them away during a meditation session or you might even want to sneak up to your bedroom and punch the hell out of a cushion for ten minutes. If no other living being sustains physical or emotional damage as a result of your actions, what harm does it do? Surely, venting your anger is a small price to pay for a healthy, happy, stress-free body.

Speak softly and carry a big stick;
you will go far.
—Theodore Roosevelt

---

d

Average shape: Sign of calm. Deals with everyday matters in a fairly rational way. Controls his temper up to the point where he can't take any more and then finally explodes. But it could be a long time coming. Agreeable, predictable, easygoing for the most part. A good level-headed person to have around.

Looped stem with tail: Handles matters in a forthright way and says whatever needs saying. Won't take any nonsense. *Fat loops*: volatile, gets angry even for small reasons; *thin loops*: shows restraint for a while, but keep pushing and eventually something's gonna give. Either way, loops mean "Get ready to run for cover."

Tiny bowl: Short fuse. Anger rises quickly but is soon over. Impatient; won't suffer fools gladly. Policy: If you've got something to say, say it and clear the air. Why hold back or beat around the bush? This person shares frustrations and disappointments openly and directly. Could afford to be more laid back and tolerant.

Large bowl: Long suffering, approachable, wants to be liked. Resentment builds slowly until it all becomes too much. May show irritation in small ways, by dropping hints or retaliating with petty gestures. Such a person could be seething inside, but you'd never know. People may take advantage of his good nature.

Scorpion: Look out for the sting in the tail! This person is never short of a witty or even cruel comment. Will always have the last word in an argument and leave you thinking, "Hell, I wish I'd said that!" In reality, he's scared of being hurt; needs to trust people more.

Drooping tail: Has the urge to say something sharp or witty, but is learning to hold back and bite his tongue rather than risk hurting others. Increasing self-esteem has led to more give-and-take. Content to win the war rather than every battle along the way.

Bloated tail: May have many fine points, but watch out for the downside! Can get very angry and defensive. The tail is saying, "Don't mess with me!" Has a lot of pent-up grievances that need releasing, but you may not want to be there when they are!

Deflected sting: Blames others when things go wrong and can even be a bit sneaky sometimes. Pulls rank, takes the moral high ground. Uses rules and orders to justify behavior. Feels let down by other people's incompetence. Would benefit by becoming more self-reliant.

Oversized: Defensive. A profound sense of injustice, rooted in childhood, underpins actions. Trouble with parents or figures of authority as a child has left him feeling bruised and hard-done-by. Small problems provoke big reactions. Sensitive, even shy, but also unpredictable.

Dislocated: Not easy to figure out. There's a whole lot going on under the surface. Keeps real problems and deeper resentments out of sight. May not be facing up to emotional issues. The strain is beginning to show.

Covered: Puts brave face on wounded feelings. Seeks to appear strong and sturdy. During difficult times he won't allow others to see how hurt or disturbed he is. Tries to brush aside criticism and damaging comments, but pain goes deeper than it appears.

Blowing away: Shrugs off pain and anger. He may be annoyed or upset, but those feelings will rarely be put into words. Would rather conceal wounds or brush them aside than get into long, involved conversations about the cause.

Tucked under: Stands up for his rights when situations aren't fair. Points out injustices and fights his corner until a compromise is reached. Not afraid to set the record straight and tell others they have acted wrongly. Anger is channeled into positive action.

Plain, looped stem: This person has a point to make, perhaps even several points. It all depends on the size of that loop. The fatter it is, the more grievances he has boiling up inside. They may explode in an angry outburst or trickle out in calm and open discussion, but they've got to come out somehow.

Plunging stem: Frustrated by arguments about issues of principle or things that simply don't matter. Petty or irrelevant disputes take up too much time. The writer knows what is important and has a strong sense of direction, but this can get knocked off balance in everyday life.

Open-backed: Unsure which issues matter most. Too much is going on to really get a focus. One day this person is wound up over something that seems important, the next he has to let that go because another matter has grabbed his attention. Grievances are shifting and uncertain.

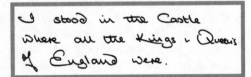

A perfect example of the Scorpion d, with its stinging tail poised and ready to strike. This person is a master of the scathing put-down. He must have the last word always, and usually that word will be witty and very sharp. Get ready to run!

e

The *e* is bursting with personality. It shows whether the writer is fun, with a good sense of humor, or quite a serious-minded character. Plus, it reveals what's going on behind the smile. Is this person really happy inside or just pretending?

a sense of humor

Humor is probably the greatest human asset of them all. For a start, it's what keeps most of us sane, particularly through those dark and difficult times in life when, if we didn't stand back and laugh at our troubles, we'd burst into tears, or much worse! I've been right down there on more occasions than I care to think about—I'm sure you have too—and as I remember it, it was usually laughter that saved the day.

Humor is the best antidote to pessimism, fear and depression I can think of. It not only lends weight to our reserves of courage and determination, but it also puts valuable distance between us and the problems we face, helping us get a fresh perspective on the things that really matter in life. Most of us take it all too seriously anyway. We know we shouldn't—the experts keep telling us that stress is bad for us—yet we just can't help "sweating the small stuff" sometimes, allowing tiny, insignificant molehills to grow into great big mountains blocking our path.

A cheerful heart can never be crushed by adversity. It will always find some ray of sunlight among the gloom, some reason to be happy. Laughter generates all sorts of physiological side effects we're not even aware of. When we smile we actually start to feel better within ourselves—and if, somehow, we can project that warmth toward other people, they pick up on our confidence and reflect it right back at us. Very soon we feel better because—well, because we *decided* to.

Remember, happiness is a choice you make. It works from the inside out every time, never the other way around.

Everything is funny as long as
it is happening to someone else.
—Will Rogers

---

e

Smiling: Upbeat personality. Amusing, chatty, likable and friendly. This person probably socializes well, so people enjoy having him around. Likes sharing jokes with friends. May not always be in the mood for a laugh, but when he is, he's great fun and contributes much to the conversation, helping create a good atmosphere.

Clenched: This writer's smile disguises a more thoughtful approach. A certain amount of tension and seriousness underlies character. Not to be underestimated. Part of his personality is for show; behind the mask lurks a less buoyant person who's often quite hard to understand. Try not to judge him on first impressions.

Too big: Really wants to be liked and accepted. Sensitive and vulnerable. Will make an effort to please others and win their favors. Longs to be part of the gang, and this may override many personal considerations. Always looking for appreciation and endorsement. Needs to start valuing himself more before other people will.

Too small: Sign of an analytical mind. Low-key personality—pleasant and friendly enough, but not always very warm. Enjoys small talk and may be good fun in a localized way, but confidence varies and the full personality may not come across. Underlying fear of embarrassment. More upbeat than he appears.

Backswing: Good sense of humor. Enjoys laughing and generally sees the funny side of life. He can take a joke and may be quite self-deprecating, even to the point of making fun of himself and the situations he gets into.

High tail: A real individual, with his own special brand of humor. He laughs at others, but can he take a joke about himself? I wouldn't bank on it! Could be defensive and scared of looking foolish. May hide strong words behind a joke or a smile, but he'll expect you to get the message.

Small fork: Fun-loving and maybe even charming too, but watch out for his mean-spirited side. Appearances are deceptive. In a fight this person could be hard to handle. Reacts badly to being cornered, let down or rejected. Don't expect to be let off lightly.

Uneven: Alarmed at how certain parts of his life are going right now. Feels uneasy about specific situations. Certain elements are out of control, and he senses that he's losing ground. Needs to get a grip and take the initiative. Don't let fear or doubt stand in the way of effective action.

Extended across: A joker who likes a laugh but often at other people's expense. Enjoys poking fun, picking up on all your silly weaknesses and mistakes, though usually without malice. Can certainly dish it out, but won't like taking it.

Extended down: Always ready to see the funny side of a difficult situation. The more hopeless things become the funnier they seem. His logic: "Let's face it, if you didn't laugh you'd cry." A good friend to help you through a crisis. Sees life as a game, not to be taken too seriously.

Lamb chop: Feels slightly awkward with his own personality. He seems fun and friendly, but what else is going on behind that smile? Expect a resourceful, smart character, someone who is a little wary of strangers and suspicious of other people's motives.

Stretched up: This writer is probably struggling at the moment. Horrified by many aspects of life, he's feeling out of step, afraid of what might happen next. People and situations have consistently let him down; now he doesn't know which way to turn. Needs to calm down and take stock.

Quick jotted note. This person has a great sense of humor. You can tell from his bright, smiley e's that he likes to laugh and enjoys a joke and, though rather pushy and demanding (see D), would be quite a fun person to have around.

f

When you're talking about making the right impression, no letter of the alphabet reveals quite as much as the *f*. So, is the writer loud and bubbly, a real life-and-soul-of-the-party type, or shy and quiet? The *f* measures how outgoing someone is and how much he cares what people think of his behavior.

making the right impression

A writer who feels self-conscious and shy when he's around other people will probably draw a large forward loop on the upper part of his *f* (see page 32). Take note of that loop: It's packed with dozens of tiny thoughts and worries. He's convinced that his friends, neighbors, even his colleagues at work are all making comments about him behind his back, criticizing the way he dresses, the color he's painted his house, the kind of newspaper he reads, etc. In fact, he's so scared of creating a bad impression that he continually adjusts his behavior to please them. Nothing is ever done without first asking, "What will people think if. . . ?" It's a pointless exercise leading to dissatisfaction, frustration and defeat.

The moment we allow external opinion to drive our actions and decisions, that's the point where we lose control of our own destiny and hand over a gigantic chunk of our free will to an invisible committee. As Mark Twain said, "We cannot reach old age by another man's road." You simply have to be yourself at every turn. Most people are not judging or criticizing you anyway. They're too caught up in their own world to care what you get up to in yours. And even if they are thinking about you, you can't be sure *what* they're thinking. Who knows, rather than condemning you, they might actually be singing your praises, saying how much they like the way you dress or what a great color your house is painted. You'll never be sure, so why worry?

Better by far to behave exactly how you want to behave and let other folk say whatever they darned well please, the way Large Lower Loop people do (again, see page 32). If others disapprove, accept that they're entitled to their opinion and ignore them; get on with enjoying yourself. Be respectful of their space and comfort, but after that, if you're having fun and nobody's getting hurt, why lose sleep over it?

Seize from every moment its unique novelty
and do not prepare your joys.
—André Gide

---

f

Loops top and bottom: A balanced view. Cares what other folk think, but not enough to change behavior to make them happy. Can be fairly outgoing and fun but without having to show off too much or come on too strong. Restrained. Has a certain style and attitude—but not enough to cause a stir.

Top loop only: His head is full of concerns and doubts, which may get in the way of a good time. Inside, not blessed with a big personality. Wants others to respect and appreciate him but suspects they won't, so he tries to make a good impression as a way of hiding any inadequacy. He fears that one day he may be found out.

Bottom loop only: Good personality, plenty to say, lively and fun in the right company. Shrugs off others' opinions: "Who cares what people think—let's party!" In full flow, can make any event go with a swing. Lights, camera, action! The bigger the loop, the bigger the personality.

Fold-over: Writer hides real self with a public mask. Wants to be seen in a certain way and tries to mold his image so that people will appreciate him, doing whatever it takes to make the desired impression. Underneath, insecure about either looks or personality. May be judgmental of others as a defense against attack.

Sharp bottom loop: Likes to have a good time. Any occasion will do. "Just gimme those invitations!" Wants to be where the action is, right there in the thick of it, seeing and being seen. Gets a kick out of dressing up and going somewhere special. Or is he simply afraid of being alone?

Stem pulled back: Prefers intimate conversations to big gatherings. Underneath, he may crave the occasional party but that's not where his heart is. There is a lot on his mind and plenty of serious things to be said. Generally, will shy away from bright lights and loud music.

Straight crossbars: Simple, straightforward tastes. Gets his kicks swapping ideas and feelings. Expresses opinions well and makes friends through common interests. You know where you stand with this person. Uncomplicated, direct, genuine.

Overhanging: Wants to be accepted, but finds it difficult to mingle. An outsider who fears that other people are having a better time than he is. Past experiences confuse issues and put thoughts in his head that shouldn't be there. Nothing is ever as simple as it should be.

Backward crossbars: Will shine only in the right environment. Too shy to really push himself forward, too self-conscious to dominate the conversation. Only emerges from his shell when he's ready and when he believes his personality will be respected and enjoyed.

letting go of the past

Growing up is never a benign, passive process. We accumulate a thousand joys and a thousand tiny hurts and injustices along the road, every one of them leaving its mark, shaping our attitudes, our behavior, and therefore our handwriting, in some significant way.

Life is designed to test the spirit, and to do so it presents us with some extremely difficult situations. Often, if we take a closer look, it's really the same situation haunting us, one that keeps on recurring over and over, each time in a slightly different form, until we pluck up the courage to tackle the underlying problem and sort it out. Whatever our particular issue may be, whether it's abuse, bullying, persistent financial troubles, a cheating partner or something else, each time we come face to face with it we are standing at a familiar crossroads. "So, are you going to stand and fight this time?" a voice asks. "Tackle this problem once and for all? Or give in and go under like you always do—defeated, unable to cope?" Plenty of people are big on coping, but to me it's a bit like boarding up your windows in the path of a hurricane and praying the storm winds will leave your house untouched. That's not how it works.

These issues need resolving. To put a stop to a recurring situation you have to dig down deep to the root cause of it. Ask simple, direct questions: Why do these things keep happening to me? What is life trying to tell me? What must I learn from this? Counseling or therapy can help, but in the end it is our own responsibility, nobody else's. Painful situations happen for a reason; they are there to teach us a major life lesson, something vital to our personal development. So stand firm and stare those demons right in the eye. The time has come to learn your lesson and move on.

Everything we shut our eyes to,
everything we run away from,
everything we deny, denigrate or despise,
serves to defeat us in the end.
—Henry Miller

---

g

Check out the tail on the g. Ask, "Which way does it swing?" The tail can be sharp and threatening, showing an angry nature, a person still working through old pain, or it can be gentle, which happens when the writer is either not angry at all or has managed to turn his back on the past.

Loop on tail: Not likely to keep problems buried inside for long. If there are issues in his life, this writer is probably handling them maturely. A small loop means problems have been dealt with and things are slowly being worked out. A large loop points to emotional matters that still need addressing and sorting out.

Open tail: Believes in dealing with problems as they come up. Won't usually allow anger to accumulate long term. Thinks, What's the point of hanging on to pain? Such an attitude may result from not having experienced deep emotional hurt in the first place, or from being thick-skinned. Determined not to appear weak.

Fierce: Sharp tail indicates bullish character, always ready for a fight. Can't watch injustice and just accept it. Has aggressive, competitive edge and an underlying anger, plus a need to prove his point and not be trampled underfoot. Probably making up for injustices felt in youth. Finally, the worm has turned!

Inward-pointing finger: Sensitive to adverse comments. Says, "Don't blame me." Believes he has given his best, so when things go wrong he finds it hard to accept blame or responsibility. Will be defensive if he stands accused. Others have to be tactful. May have been wrongly taken to task as a child.

No loop: Quite even-tempered, with few traces of pain or hidden anger. May just be naïve and lack experience or may not see the point of hanging on to old grievances. Instead, prefers to lay them to rest and move on. Sees reason when others don't. Calm and reassuring.

Small head, jabbing tail: Prone to outbursts of spontaneous anger. No lasting resentment, though. Just yells and says what must be said, however harsh it might be. Then the fury dissolves and everything is bright and sunny again. Anger is fierce but fleeting.

Small head, with loop: There is a degree of intolerance here. Aware of his duty to the folks around him and tries to live up to it, but personal concerns are also very important. People only complicate matters, distracting from the writer's own priorities. Quite tense inside.

Closed: Expect the sulks! This person was probably a spoiled child who never really grew up. Plays the role of victim, whimpering after a dispute, lapping up every last drop of drama. Really it's a crafty ploy to get attention and make others feel guilty.

Big and looped: Many troublesome issues remain unresolved from years ago. Wounds still haven't healed. Heightened sensitivity means he takes offense easily and often sets himself up to get hurt. Any outer strength is hiding a much weaker interior. Needs to tackle outstanding conflicts and finally lay them to rest.

Open-backed: He's never quite sure how anger should be expressed, so it leaks out at all the wrong times in all the wrong places. Resentment is being contained rather than being channeled in the right direction at the people who have hurt his feelings.

Hooded: Thick-skinned. He may seem tough but he's not really. The outer shell hides a softer, more vulnerable interior, if only he'd show it! He doesn't want to appear weak and risk getting hurt again, so he's erected barricades to keep the "enemy" out. Could afford to ease up a little.

Stretched up: Feels hurt, but is determined to be brave and soldier on regardless, as though it doesn't matter. In some ways, he likes others to witness the suffering and see the damage they've caused. That way they share his pain. But can he bring himself to reveal how hurt he really is?

Large pointed lip: Continually fighting off attack with sharp words and displays of temper. It's a strain. Assaults may be imagined. The writer is dealing with many personal issues and concerns and is not ready for others to challenge his position. Defensive, unsettled.

Rounded lip: Expects others to see reason and believes his arguments are clear and obvious, but sometimes he does not tell the whole story, so others don't quite get the picture. The need for understanding runs deep, and so too does his frustration at being misunderstood.

Sweeping under: Some things are spoken about, others remain hidden away. This person may get angry with people over small and, as they see it, insignificant, things, but there is more to his actions and motives than meets the eye—a vast reservoir of secret thoughts and feelings.

Bela Lugosi's signature. Packed with all the high drama and elegance you might expect from a star of old-style horror movies. The large loop on the g contains so much raw emotion. This was a man who felt pain deeply, and showed it too, in grand, attention-grabbing gestures. A larger-than-life display!

h

This is how we measure spiritual fulfillment. Has the writer figured out what life is all about and why we're here? How deep is his understanding of his relation to the universe? Does he believe in his own amazing potential as a unique individual or just follow the crowd and take on the same beliefs as everybody else?

faith and believing

To have faith means having a simple yet deep trust that everything in your life is going exactly according to plan and that, however gloomy present circumstances seem to be, it'll all work out fine in the end—in fact, better than fine: *perfectly*, bringing you greater benefits and deeper fulfillment than you ever thought possible.

When you're confronted with bad news or some kind of rejection or just a general disheartening slump in your affairs, it's always tempting to admit defeat and give up, especially when the voices of doom around you are saying, "It's gonna get worse. You're not gonna make it!" the way voices of doom tend to. And yet with faith on your side you're able to rise above all that. Even in the most devastating crisis you can weather the storm, if you tell yourself with calm assurance that "this too shall pass." Faith takes away the urge to panic. Instead of becoming anxious, you go with the flow, changing what you can and accepting what you can't, because you've learned how everything in life goes in cycles. Just as winter doesn't last forever but must eventually loosen its grip to make way for the spring, so any bad times are sure to be temporary too.

Often, it's only when a crisis draws to a close that we really appreciate its true value. At last we see the golden thread weaving through it all, and marvel at the way the pieces fit together so intricately, how one stumbling step led to another with astonishing, almost uncanny precision. Better still, it was not the empty struggle we imagined it to be at the time, but a valuable learning experience, something that made us stronger and ready for the next stage in our personal journey.

Faith is a substance of things hoped for,
the evidence of things not seen.
—Hebrews, 11:1

---

h

Check out the height of the stem and the size of the hoop. The taller that stem is, the more idealistic the writer will be. Tall-stem people are on a personal quest. A hoop that rides high up the stem means a contented person, someone with faith in life and a greater understanding of what is possible.

Tall stem, looped: This person is idealistic. He expects a lot from life—and life had better deliver! He was raised with certain values and principles and taught to ask the question "Why?" Faith may be strong, and yet it gets distorted at times by too much thinking. Believes what he believes and won't welcome outside interference.

Low stem, looped: Sidetracked by his own doubts; may have lost his way. Seems to have stopped searching and settled for a narrow range of ideas. Caught up in too many thoughts and fears. May be defensive. Would like to believe there is something, someone, out there looking after us, but is there really? Confused.

Big hoop, small stem: Happy with life. Has a pleasantly uncomplicated view of the world, which says, "If you don't ask tricky questions, you don't have to deal with tricky answers." Prefers to enjoy what he's got rather than work out what else there might be. Simple values, simple faith.

Tiny hoop, tall stem: Highly idealistic. Follows unconventional paths without knowing where they'll lead or what they mean. Every avenue yields fresh possibilities, new questions. Lacks realism and understanding and needs to focus more and probe more deeply into life. This person is a long way away from discovering the truth.

Straight, uncomplicated: Reflects a straight, uncompli-cated view of life. Generally quite a happy individual who makes few demands and who tends to be contented with what he has right now. Sure, he'd like to receive more, but he's also grateful for what he's been given already.

Hoop hugs stem: Unadventurous. Likes what he knows and knows what he likes. This person enjoys a simple faith, but wisdom is limited. Sitting cozily inside his comfort zone, he sees no reason to go in search of new things to worry about. Limited vision. Needs to think bigger!

Curving out: Willing to share his spiritual ideas with others but unwilling to alter his ideas if others disagree with them. May not listen to opposing arguments just in case the new information conflicts with his beliefs. He's happy as he is, thank you!

Curving in: Keeps personal beliefs under wraps. Articles of faith are personal and not for sharing. He draws a line that others must not cross. Secretly, maybe not so confident about what he believes; fears that listening to opposing views might undermine his faith even more.

Pulled back: Looking for answers, but can't separate his own philosophy from the teachings of parents and others who influenced him as a child. Any scope for exploring spiritual matters is limited by this conditioning. The need to break free is weighed against a sense of loyalty to his upbringing.

Pinched hoop: Narrow vision backed by small-time understanding. Reality is cramping his style and eating away at his faith. Because of skepticism or a fear of the unknown, he remains trapped, feeling restless, even unhappy, but unsure why. Ripe for a spiritual awakening.

Hoop detached from stem: Self-reliant; someone who works out his own principles as he goes. So far he has traveled in one direction when the truth about life really lies in another. Feels he's come too far along the road to change. Still plenty of room for inner growth and self-discovery.

Stem half-looped: Unsure what he believes in. Sometimes this is caused by the writer's interests being caught up with someone else's—a partner or parents or even a group. The desire to learn and grow is there, but it is undermined by external factors that confuse the issue.

i

living in the now

"We want to live in the present," Henry Ford said. "The only history that is worth a tinker's damn is the history we make today." To feel truly alive you must invest "today" with every spark of vigor you possess. Grab your chance to shine while you can. Do it right away, for there will never be another moment like this one, so filled with promise and opportunity.

Realistically, the present moment is all we have anyway. Now. This minute. What else can there be? Yesterday is old news, tomorrow has yet to yield up its many twists and surprises; we have no choice but to do what we can where we are. That means taking a risk, being willing to engage in positive action without always being sure of the consequences, testing our capabilities to the fullest whenever we get the chance, not hanging back in case some better or safer opportunity comes along later. Play the game as if it matters, and don't sweat too much if you trip and get it wrong.

The truth is, nobody knows the steps to this dance. Nobody ever did. Not your parents, not your teachers, not the thousands of so-called experts whose views we hear so often on TV or read about in newspapers. We're all learning as we go, making it up from day to day, never doing it exactly right, never quite mastering the technique. But surely that's what makes life so much fun in the first place—the unreliability of it all, never having all the facts, never knowing what will happen next. All we *do* know is that the future and the past are both dead time. We're powerless to exist in either. So let go of them and insist on living right here, right now.

Live all you can, it's a mistake not to.
It doesn't matter so much what you do
in particular, so long as you have your life.
If you haven't had that, what have you had?
—Henry James

---

i

Check out the dot above the *i*. If the dot is to the left of the stem, then this person dwells in the past or is considering how far he has come in life. If he draws the dot to the right of the stem, his mind is fixed on future developments. A dot directly above the stem means he prefers to focus on events right here in the present.

Dot floating above stem: Fixed in the present. Able to take information from all sides and process it. Draws on influences from the past, aware of possible developments in the future, but everything is done in moderation. Doesn't get hung up on any one area. Sane, sober approach.

Dot to the left of stem: Events in the past are important. Either thinks olden days were golden days and keeps going over and over old situations, or is just fascinated by history—general, family or personal. Whatever the case, it distracts from enjoyment of the present. The farther to the left the dot is, the truer this may be.

Dot to the right of the stem: Future plans and developments are what matter here. The way things are going, how ambitions and ideas are shaping up, the effect external factors might have on his plans. Can't enjoy present circumstances for worrying about the future. The farther to the right the dot is, the truer this will be.

Dot close to stem: Attention focused right in the now, possibly too much so. This person's own concerns predominate and all efforts are geared toward personal needs and desires. Nothing else matters. May be selfish or obsessed with detail. Either way, he's missing the bigger picture and probably losing ground.

High dot: Maintains an excellent overview of business and what's going on. Keeps many factors in his sights. Constantly reviewing his position and evaluating strengths and weaknesses of the present situation. Efficient.

Streaked dot: This person is worried about the future and how upcoming developments will impact his status and current concerns. Has a fear of the unknown and of losing control. Needs to do his very best in the present and leave the future to take care of itself. Have confidence.

Circle dot: An innocent lamb. Naïve, young at heart, someone who refuses to grow up. By choice or by circumstance, this writer has not become hardened or cynical. Views people and the world with a positive expectation and reaps rewards accordingly.

No dot: Can't think of one thing for thinking of another. The mind is all over the place—past, present and future. There is too much going on, with many demands on his time and energy. Jobs may only be half done in the rush. Needs a vacation.

Arrow-dot: Aware, alert and anxious. Always checking details, sifting through information. Probably quite scrupulous, too. Fears intrusion by others and the consequences of mistakes. Could even be neurotic. Focuses on the present to prevent things going wrong in the future.

Dash for dot: Territorial. A lot of energy goes into preserving the current position. There is a deep need inside this person to keep things as they are and to protect himself from (imaginary) threats from outside. By closing up, resisting change, he is resisting the pull of destiny.

Al Gore must be the hottest favourite to succeed Bill Clinton than any previous Vice-President of the United States.

Seriously cramped and closed handwriting, indicating someone who is in denial about many of his deeper feelings and impulses and who therefore keeps a tight control on his emotional responses. The covered dash-for-dot i's are proof of his self-control. This is someone who enjoys the status quo and doesn't want any surprises to come along and disrupt it. Self-protective and restrained.

j

Some people can't handle praise. Either they don't feel they deserve it or they treat all compliments as flattery, which they brush aside as insincere. The shape of the *j* offers clues to how modest the writer might be; is praise an unwanted bonus or does he grab every last ounce of reassurance he can get?

approval

Approval is good for us. We thrive on it. No one can resist the power of a well-timed compliment, a few kind, encouraging words delivered straight from the heart. Their effect is potent and magical. All at once the dark clouds are blown away, and we feel valued, uplifted and, more importantly, driven to do even better next time.

For that reason, it's essential that you heap praise on those you love and care about. Do it unconditionally every chance you get. Don't hold back or wait for the perfect time. *Today* is the perfect time—to praise your kids, encouraging them to succeed and prosper in any direction that is right for them; to congratulate friends on their work, their choice of clothes, their hair or the car they drive; in fact, to endorse and cherish anyone who matters to you. Do it freely and generously. Do it not for personal gain or with an eye on what you might get out of it, but because you want to and because you know it's going to make the other person feel great. If they fail to repay the compliment, well, that's okay—maybe next time. But if they do praise you in return, accept it graciously. Try not to fall into the fake-modesty trap by shrugging off their kind words, as if to say, "Me? Oh no, I'm not worthy of your attention." That's baloney. You are very special, and you're worthy of every last scrap of attention you can get your hands on! Treat it as a sign that, at long last, you're finally doing something right!

Always create an atmosphere of reward around yourself. The more praise you can lavish on others, the more you'll get back in return.

I have often wished I had time
to cultivate modesty,
but I am too busy thinking about myself.
—Edith Sitwell

---

j

Looped: Probably too modest about his own accomplishments. More likely to spread praise around: "Aw, I couldn't have done this alone. It was a team effort." All compliments must be genuine. He's got no time for cheap flattery, so don't waste your breath.

Straight down: Loves approval; actively seeks it out. Wants to know he's on the right track, that his decisions are good ones. Looking for reassurance and a pat on the back. Without it he feels insecure. To his mind, you just can't have too many compliments! He will do what it takes to earn praise and will glow when he receives it.

Curled: Enjoys a few words of praise every now and again, but it must be heartfelt and well intended. Able to distinguish between sincerity and BS. Not so easily won over by vague words of approval—must be specific. Encouragement is vital; this person will perform far better if you handle him the right way.

Big loop: Has real problems with the whole idea of approval. Probably never received much when he was young and so now it makes him uncomfortable. Even if he deserves the praise, he can't accept it. May be suspicious of your motives and become defensive. Doesn't want to hear. Confidence needs a huge boost.

Hooked inward: He just can't believe you said something nice. "Who, me? You really mean *me?*" Blushes, and gushes with false modesty. Like everyone else, this person enjoys approval, but he feels insecure and undeserving of attention.

Sweeping under: Invites praise from every side, but why? Eager for the right kind of attention; craves adoration and respect and goes to great lengths to maneuver himself into the right position to receive it. Deep inside, there are many insecurities.

Curled, with top flipper: Pretends not to need approval from anyone. He backs off almost disbelievingly, in case he's being fooled or flattered. Underneath, he wants the right kind of people to endorse him. Will he be able to accept it, though, when they do?

Sweep and curl: Friendly, open to compliments, and willing to do his best to earn them. However, the outer personality may conceal another agenda buried well out of sight. Some aspects of this person's character or motives are not being revealed. What *is* he up to?

k

From the shape of a k you can tell how loving and nurturing the writer is and whether or not he allows himself to show emotion openly; also how much affection this person seeks in return. In short, is he a giver or a taker? It's also a useful guide to how charming and persuasive he can be.

affection and charm

What could be more natural than a hug? It's one of the most rewarding physical activities there is, yet also one of the most misunderstood. Hugging is not about grabbing someone and squeezing him until he turns blue. It's a transfer of heart energy—you throw your arms around a person, he throws his arms around you, and there you both stand for a few seconds, chest to chest, exchanging several kilowatts of warmth and emotion. It's wonderful for the system.

Not everyone can handle a full embrace, however. I've met people over the years whose emotional wires were so tangled they'd rather put a live tarantula down their pants than make real physical contact with another human being, especially in public where everyone can see, and especially if it's with someone of the same sex. Crazy, isn't it? I mean, who in their right mind would let embarrassment get in the way of a good time?

When two hearts meet—literally meet, as they do when you're hugging—it causes a great rush of energy to pass between you. This is a special, reassuring moment, one that can be incredibly empowering. Hugs are a tonic, after all. They lift the spirits and cause us to feel better, not just about the person we're embracing, but also about ourselves.

Never turn down the chance to hug someone you care about. Hug 'em tight and hug 'em long. Do it with so much enthusiasm that you can feel the electric charge buzzing between the two of you. These things matter in life; they make a difference. Don't miss out.

Gather ye rosebuds while ye may,
Old time is still a-flying;
And this same flower that smiles today,
Tomorrow will be dying.
—Robert Herrick

---

k

> **Check out** the size and shape of the arms of the *k*. The longer the lower arm is, the more charming and persuasive the writer will be. But when both arms are long and outstretched it's usually a sign that he loves to give and receive affection. Hugs are definitely on the menu!

Arms outstretched: Needs affection like flowers need sunshine. Very huggable and keen to show he cares by giving attention to others. Not afraid to display emotion or to be demonstrative with those he loves. Feelings are genuine and expressed openly. Will expect similar in return, though—so get hugging!

Looped, with flipper: Likes to be kind to people and show affection, and can also be charming, up to a point. Has a rather down-to-earth, street-wise view of love. Not easily won over. Likes to set limits and see others stick to them. Affection may be mechanical sometimes, or used to achieve his own ends. Strict, but loving.

Extended lower arm: Says, "Trust me, I'm genuine," but may not be, so take extra care. Charm is used as a means to an end. Fancy words mixed with smiles and charisma present a pleasant, attractive image, but it's all a tiny bit contrived. Very aware of his own powers of persuasion. Would make a great salesperson!

Extended upper arm: Short on charm, long on laying down the law. Prefers to tell rather than be told. In relationships, could be a bit difficult or demanding. Words may contain veiled threats if the writer doesn't get his own way. Could lead to tricky situations. A taker rather than a giver. Can be hard to love sometimes.

Arms too outstretched: Very demonstrative, with a deep craving for affection. The person may appear desperate for appreciation and love. Needs could be overwhelming. Always seeking endorsement and a sense of belonging and will try any means available to earn his reward.

Small arms: Suppresses emotion due to a fear of feeling awkward or embarrassed. Has set limits to his emotional range, trapping many urges and needs inside. Keeps other people's affection at bay rather than letting them get too close.

Scissored arms: Feels uneasy with overt displays of emotion—kissing, hugging, too much attention. Either he doesn't know how to respond or he's uncomfortable with physical contact, afraid to let himself go and allow others into his personal space.

Vertical upper arm: Tough on himself and others. Behind the pleasant exterior lies a steely personality, someone with secret strengths who will use them if necessary. If that means pulling people into line, then fine. One mistake could cost you dearly.

Sharp lower arm: Impatient. Tells it like it is. Takes no nonsense. Gets to the point and so should you. The time he spent at charm school had no effect! He has definite demands and expectations, and others had better live up to them, otherwise there could be trouble.

Disconnected arms: Insincere and schmoozy. He says "Stay in touch," but won't return your calls. She says "You're absolutely adorable—let's do lunch sometime," and never speaks to you again. Showing affection is a social grace and means nothing. Don't fall under the spell.

Tall stem: Idealistic about love. Expects big things from affectionate exchanges, but is rarely satisfied by the outcome. Other people seldom live up to their promises. This person no doubt believes that love conquers all, and so despairs when others don't feel the same way.

Arms stretch beyond stem: Hugs come with strings attached. Has a deep hunger for love that can never be satisfied. Yearns to be cherished, never feels valued in the right way. There is a hole somewhere. Needs to pin down the cause: Resolve any conflict with parents and start over.

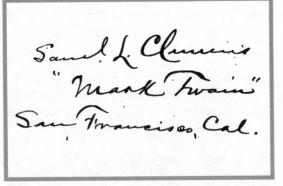

Signature of **Samuel Langhorne Clemens**, *alias* **Mark Twain**.
The lower arm on his k *shows how persuasive this man could be. He could charm the birds out of the trees when he put his mind to it. But appearances can be deceptive. He was really a lot less outgoing and good humored under the surface.*

1

An *l* describes how single-minded a person tends to be in pursuit of his ambitions. Those ambitions don't have to be too grand or elaborate; they could be simple goals for a life of steady achievement. Whatever his plans or dreams, though, the *l* shows us how keen the writer is to achieve them.

ambition—the will to strive and succeed

Each one of us is capable of many great things, in most cases far greater than ever we imagine, yet too often we fall short of our true potential. Because of fear or low self-confidence or even laziness, we end up settling for less than we deserve. Many people with singular gifts and abilities that, if applied diligently and with courage, would lift them to the very top of their chosen profession, throw it all away before they've even started. They aim too low, afraid to take a chance, scared to dream big dreams and shoot for the moon the way others do, in case they overstretch themselves and fall back down to earth again with a humiliating bump.

For a select few, however, the ever-present risk of failure is counterbalanced by the even greater risk that *they might succeed*. To them, anything is possible. Although they may have exactly the same quota of abilities as the others, their attitude is different: They're ready to get out there and channel those abilities, seizing every opportunity they can to thrive and grow and prove themselves to the world. And because they won't allow their mind to be darkened by self-doubt or pessimism but instead keep pressing on until they accomplish what they set out to do, they invariably finish somewhere near the top of the heap. It's no surprise. They believed they could do it and they simply proved themselves right.

However grand or modest your ambitions may be, whether your aim is to be the best homemaker, the best student, the best salesperson in your company, or to cultivate the finest garden in your neighborhood, all that is asked of you is that you commit wholeheartedly to doing your best. Anticipate only triumph in your endeavors; accept that nothing less will do. Rise above your fears and any perceived limitations. If you feel you're settling for less than you deserve, be willing to change. Decide that the time has come to start turning a few of those old neglected dreams into a glorious reality. Then go for it.

Whatever you can do, or dream you can, begin it.
Boldness has genius, power and magic in it.
— Goethe

1

> ✐ **Check out** the height of the *l*. A tall *l* means the writer has a clear idea what he wants and is single-minded in the pursuit of his dreams. The smaller and stumpier that *l* becomes, the less well defined the goals. He may know he wants more out of life, but so far he hasn't worked out what the "more" might be.

Strong, tall, with small or no loop: Someone who takes goals seriously and pursues them single-mindedly. Always rises to the occasion and expects others to do the same. Frustrated by low achievers. Success may come, but at what cost? Needs to remember: The aim is to live long *and* wide!

Tall, with loop: Goals and dreams often outstrip this person's talent for achieving them, but that won't stop him trying. He surprises himself and others by achieving the impossible. Begins tasks without always knowing whether he will make the grade. Curiously, his efforts pay off and he makes it by the skin of his teeth! Smart.

Small, stumpy: Modest aims backed by low-octane personality; lacks the drive to achieve. May fall into the right niche rather than actively pursuing any particular one. Whatever he's done so far, it is only a fraction of what is possible. Needs to reconsider life goals, otherwise the present way of life could lead to frustration later.

Split up the middle: Inner conflict. The writer has his own ambitions and dreams, but external influences—parents, teachers, partners or just his background generally—have cramped his style. Uncertainty hinders progress toward true fulfillment. Should follow his heart and ignore all unsolicited advice.

Curved back: Past teachings and influences cloud judgment or reduce effectiveness. This person feels he's being pulled in two different directions and has compromised too much, settling for less than he really deserves. Time to break free and be true to himself.

Short, fat: Works feverishly in the short term because he fears losing out in the long term. Possibly a greedy individual. Inside, he feels unsure of himself and his abilities, so he tries too hard. It's a way of compensating for insecurities. Should slow down, take time to smell the roses.

Large looped: Plenty going on here. Perhaps too much! Mind is cluttered with so many thoughts and desires. Believes that anything can be achieved if he puts his mind to it, but what should he do first? Answer: prioritize. Do less thinking, be more focused in the action taken.

Way too tall: Builds castles in the air. Impractical view of his own talents. There is no point in being single-minded and having a goal if that goal is unattainable. Needs grounding. Would benefit from being more realistic and building solid foundations.

Drooping: Often the sign of a recent career setback. Unsinkable plans may have developed a leak. Despite all his efforts and faith, his dreams have come unstuck and he has begun to lose hope. It's only temporary. Things will change. Confidence has taken a knock, needs boosting.

Floating high: A dreamer who is being grounded by the folks around him. His desire to think big thoughts, run away from reality, or achieve certain goals without first laying strong foundations is almost overwhelming. Needs to take a more down-to-earth view of his abilities.

Tall double-l: Quite satisfied with progress at present. Has achieved what he set out to do, with lots more on the way. Here's someone who has made his dreams come true, often against the odds, and is unstoppable in his pursuit of future goals. Good prospects.

Stumpy double-l: Either frustrated at work and looking for new ways to move forward, or he has gone as high as it's possible to go. Whichever it is, this person has capabilities beyond his present position and is not living up to his potential. Why not?

Left stumpy, right tall: On the outside, this person may appear fulfilled and happy, but inside he has a sense of frustration, of going nowhere fast. His actions are not supported by confidence and faith. His career has taken a wrong turn. True happiness lies elsewhere.

Left straight, right split: Stressed. The writer feels secure about his career, but can't take a long-term view due to short-term problems. Each day brings fresh crises; just dealing with these takes all his energy. Needs to find the time to gather his thoughts and make new plans.

> I've booked the ticket for Friday night and we can pick them up at the door. See You at the tube as arranged at about 7pm – if I'm running late I'll call you on your mobile.
> See You Soon X

Strong, single-minded, ambitious. This woman's l's may look small, but compared to the rest of the writing you notice they're quite large. The tall single-l in "late" is a sign of her ability to set goals and achieve them through persistent effort, while her tall double-l's, in "I'll," though indicating a bit of stress, tell us she is fulfilled by her work and progressing well.

m

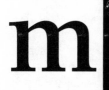

The *m* can be used to measure the balance of power within any relationship. It tells us which partner dominates and who puts more effort into keeping the show on the road. It is also a pretty good way to tell if one of them is having a serious affair on the side!

balance within relationships

True balance is hard to achieve in almost any situation in life, but nowhere more so than between partners in a loving relationship. Once the honeymoon period is over, that's the point when reality begins to set in, and it's not unusual to uncover quite a few rough edges that need smoothing out. No doubt the *intention* in most cases is to achieve a level of equality and balance where both sides respect one another's space and freedom and neither one dominates—and in a perfect world that's how it should be—but realistically, this is just not possible. No two individuals are ever exactly equal, no matter how hard they try to be. In the end one of them usually ends up being the driving force and motivator and setting the pace for the entire relationship.

Of course, if both sides accept this imbalance, there's nothing to worry about; the bond should survive okay. If they don't, it spells trouble. We are all separate beings in our own right, each with our own specific rules and boundaries and needs; none of us has the right to impose our will on anybody else—not at home, not at work, not anywhere—nor should we have to submit to bullying tactics ourselves, even if we happen to love the person who's doing the bullying. Whether you've been in a relationship for five months or fifty years, you have a duty to remain true to yourself and stay master of your own destiny.

Sharing our life with someone special does not mean giving up our individuality along with it, or that we have to sacrifice our dreams simply because our partner doesn't happen to agree with them. We should be aiming for balance, ready to be fair and willing to compromise when it really counts, but we must also remain true to our purpose at all times and insist on doing what is right.

Marriage is a wonderful thing.
But then again, so is a bicycle repair kit.
—Billy Connolly

---

m

Check out the size of the hoops on the *m*. Ask: Which hoop is larger—right or left? The left hoop represents the writer and the right one his or her partner. Whichever is bigger, that's the person who dominates the relationship and sets the pace from day to day.

Same-sized hoops, with flippers: This is someone who is very actively involved in the relationship. The hoops point to a mutually respectful couple, where neither dominates and each is allowed his or her say. Cultural influences dictate standards. These two may complain about each other, but there is a loving bond here.

Same-sized hoops, no flippers: Balanced relationship with neither side taking the lead. Both partners work to their own strengths and rely on the love and support of each other to make up for any weaknesses. Not fiery or volatile. There is mutual understanding—compromise backed by a desire to make it work out.

Large left hoop: The writer is the dominant half. It may be because a weak partner allows him or her to be, or there may be a more specific reason; such as the partner is unwell and needs care and support. (Or maybe there is no significant other currently). Lacks balance; could cause problems if level of control is not agreed upon beforehand.

Large right hoop: Writer's partner dominates. For whatever reason, the writer is allowing his or her lover to call the shots and make many of the important decisions. There could be an element of hero-worship here; may place too much trust in partner. Needs to be less dependent and more assertive.

Tiny: Where's the fun? Lacks exuberance and big-time passion. Love is generally a low-key affair. If the current relationship began with a bang, it's now coasting along with the occasional whimper. Perhaps a second honeymoon is needed to revive the spirit.

High left stem: This person brings strong standards to relationships. Lasting values and principles set by parents take precedence over his own views. Expects partner to live up to them—or else. The higher that stem rises, the more rigid and pronounced the standards will be.

No right hoop: Probably no partner currently. There is an imbalance here; any relationship is weighted in favor of the writer. Alternatively, either he has not struck lucky yet and found the perfect person, or his partner has made an exit for whatever reason. Be tactful when asking.

Jagged: A bit immature, too controlled. Feels unable to let go and allow the relationship to develop naturally. Due to inexperience or an unwillingness to experiment, this person has fixed ideas of how he and any partner should behave. Cracks could show under pressure.

Three hoops: The writer may be sharing his life with two lovers at the same time. He feels pulled two ways and is unable to make 100 percent commitment to either one. Although he cares about both, he can't bring himself to make a choice. Sounds like a recipe for trouble.

Separate hoops: There is a distance between the partners. Two people sharing a home life but doing their own thing for the rest of the time. Each person has his or her freedom, but at the expense of real closeness. It's often the best way, but could be difficult for some.

n

This letter keeps dark secrets locked away deep inside. The *n* is our guide to whether a person is open and approachable or private and guarded. How much information does he give away about himself? How long will it take to really get to know what he's like? A week? A year?

privacy

The most interesting people to hang out with, I find, are not the ones who insist on filling you in on every last detail of their life, but those who make a point of keeping their private side private. The less you know about them, the more intriguing they become. All the important stuff—details of their personal life, news about the latest project they're working on, their plans for the future, anything that is nobody else's business but their own—is kept where it belongs: under wraps. Why? Because long ago they learned a very simple lesson of life: to play their cards close to their chest and never, ever reveal what they're going to do—until they've done it. In other words, the message is: Zip your lip!

The moment you go broadcasting your ideas and plans all about the place, you sabotage them. The more you talk and the more you boast, the more you burn off the energy that would otherwise be channeled into achieving your goal. Very soon, you find the concept has gone stale and you've talked the life right out of it. Better instead to keep your own counsel. Say as little as possible as rarely as possible.

However, if you really must talk about your plans to someone, be sure to choose your allies with great care. Only share your thoughts with those who you know will support and encourage you. If you give the wet blankets ammunition against you, don't be surprised if they do what wet blankets like to do: try to throw you off course with words of doubt and discouragement. When you believe in your ideas and you sense intuitively that you are on the right track, you must have the confidence to back them yourself all the way. Be bold, be enthusiastic, but above all, whenever possible, be quiet.

You can't build a reputation on what you're going to do.
—Henry Ford

---

n

Hooped: Won't give much away, so you'll never know the whole story. Won't enjoy being probed, either. A private individual, guarded about many aspects of his life. May not be secretive or mysterious, but the longer you know him, the more he will surprise you with his depth and insights.

Sprawling: Tells you his whole life story, often without being prompted. Always open and approachable. Thinks: What's the point of hiding anything? Shares opinions and finer details of personal life with anyone who will listen. May be shallow, or may lack confidence and crave attention. Either way, good fun.

Plunging: Keeps himself very much to himself. Doesn't want anyone to lift the veil and peer inside his mind. Protects information, personal dreams and desires; may even keep them under mental lock and key. Guarded, concerned to maintain an air of intrigue. Not the easiest person to get to know.

Hooped, with flipper: Contrary. Wants you to be interested in the workings of his mind, but likes to retain a spirit of intrigue, too. Self-reliant and private, but not so much that others aren't welcome to take a lively interest. May spread disinformation about himself to keep friends and colleagues from knowing the real truth.

Very large: Private thoughts run deeper than you might think. Beneath the immature, shy or even defensive exterior lies a maze of unsolved puzzles and many personal questions still waiting to be asked. In some ways, this person is keeping full-bloom adulthood at arm's length.

Pinched: Deceptively intense. Focuses on a narrow band of private troubles, which he is slow to share with others. Inside, could be hurting badly or be worried about life, but it could be difficult to pin down one specific cause.

Hooped, but simple: Stays silent about private issues as a matter of courtesy or just through habit. Slow to open up about personal affairs. Tells you what you need to know and no more. Has no desire to share private insights with the whole world.

Suspension bridge: Very open and accessible. Has nothing to hide, shares everything with everyone. Transparent and up-front, perhaps even rather shallow and gossipy. Sees no reason to conceal the truth about himself; gets frustrated when others have secrets and won't tell.

Stretched up: Secretive about many small things. They may not be interconnected and probably won't seem important to the outside world, but he doesn't care—he just likes to keep certain parts of his life out of the spotlight. Probe too deep and he will become evasive and shy away.

Hooped but tiny: What he considers private may not be of interest to anyone but himself anyway. Just naturally protective of his affairs. Some might say he has something to hide, but he believes these little secrets add intrigue to his personality.

Crooked: Shy. This shyness may be real, but it is equally likely to be just an affectation. Likes to be coy about many of his ideas, plans, thoughts and dreams. Enjoys tantalizing others and likes the thrill of the chase as they try to guess what he's really about.

Looped: Wheels within wheels. Somewhere behind this person's private nature lies a number of questions and doubts that have never been brought to light or fully explained away. Insecurities lurk unseen, covered up and forgotten about. Any demons must be exorcised.

Compressed: The writer has retreated to a defensive position in order to keep the world at bay. Perhaps circumstances have driven him back under pressure. Now, to a certain extent, he wishes he could be left alone to carry on his life in peace.

Best wishes and good luck.

Rodolph Valentino

Rodolph Valentino. *Clearly a sensitive, kind and graceful man, but also highly demanding, both on himself and others. The n in "and" shows what an approachable person he was—willing to share his feelings and his ideas with others at the drop of a hat. This guy was an open book.*

Jane Doe
555 - 1212
35 Cresent Lane
Youngstown, Ohio

A private n. This is a woman who keeps her affairs to herself. She tells people what they need to know and no more. Those tall, narrow n's show she has many secrets on many different levels. One could know her quite well and yet not really know her at all.

generosity

No selfless act of generosity ever goes unrewarded. You've heard it said many times, I'm sure: "What goes around comes around." In other words, whatever you put out, eventually you get back again, not just in the original amount but multiplied.

To receive an abundance of money in the future, for example, you must first relax your grip on whatever money you have right now. Don't hoard it, or hang on to every last penny in case your supply dries up. A fear of poverty only draws the reality of poverty that much closer. Instead, spend your money fearlessly, and give it generously—believing, *knowing*, as you do so that what you put out must surely come right back at you, abundantly and in perfect ways. Not tomorrow perhaps, not even next month, but *it will come*, you can be sure of it, often through the most unforeseen channels.

When you give selflessly—and we're not just talking in terms of money here, but anything—love, encouragement, support—by that very act you set invisible wheels in motion. Like some vast universal accounting system working away unseen in the background, these ensure that no score ever goes unsettled. Even the most trivial good deed is paid back in kind. Love is rewarded with love, affection with affection, friendship with friendship—always provided you give with the right motive. If you give begrudgingly or with one eye on the spoils (i.e., on what you might eventually get out of it), your ticket to riches is canceled on the spot. Selfless giving has to be an act of faith, done with no thought of gain. That way, you open the door for miracles to happen. Instead of finishing with less money like you feared, you find yourself with more, and often *far* more than you ever gave away. I've never known this to fail. Trust it, rely on it and give freely with no thought for what your reward might be. Just know that whatever is due to you, you'll receive, at the perfect time and in perfect ways—100 percent guaranteed.

We must not only give what we have, we must also give what we are.
—Cardinal Mercier

O

Check out the roundness of the *o*. Generally, the rounder and larger it is, the more giving and caring the writer is likely to be. A small, tight *o* suggests meanness or at least a level of shrewdness that cancels out any chance of spontaneous giving—not just financially but in other areas of life, too: love, encouragement, etc.

Circular, plain: The writer loves to give and to receive. There is sensitivity and openness, even innocence here, which makes him accessible, generous and not the sort to hang on to his cash selfishly. This person has a kind, caring side, which shows up in all kinds of heartfelt gestures. He can expect to receive many good things out of life.

Small, tight: Possible sign of meanness or, at the very least, that he tends to be shrewd and know how to hang on to what he's got. Holds back, analyzes and appears withdrawn or possibly calculating. Not comfortable allowing his weaker side to show. This person associates fearless giving with losing or acting rashly. Circumspect, questioning and prudent.

With top tail: Protects own interests and is ready to fend off anyone trying to exploit his good nature. Believes in making money but also in protecting it. May be too aware of the value of cash to part with it. Same could apply to emotional life, relationships, bonds with friends, etc. A guarded heart and closed wallet block the channels to greater abundance.

Looped: Loops spell reservations. The loop inside the *o* shows how much of himself and his resources the writer is willing to share. Giving is geared to circumstances; everything is relative. Never goes the whole way—won't love enough, or let go enough, or be adventurous enough. May seem generous, but will usually act in his own best interests.

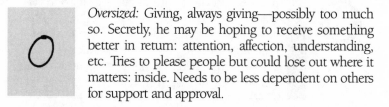

Oversized: Giving, always giving—possibly too much so. Secretly, he may be hoping to receive something better in return: attention, affection, understanding, etc. Tries to please people but could lose out where it matters: inside. Needs to be less dependent on others for support and approval.

Capped: Fears personal loss, so holds back and won't give freely until many questions have been asked. Past hurt has left its scars, and he's determined not to fall for the old tricks again. Much is going on behind the scenes. Could be rather selfish.

Elongated: Fraught, restricted; resources are stretched and nerves, too. Doesn't give enough. Would like to, but doesn't know how. The moment never seems right. Not sure how others will respond. Feels that others are ungrateful and therefore hesitates before giving.

Leaning back: If *o* hugs the previous letter, the writer's decisions always need backup and support. He rarely feels comfortable acting alone. He wants to know he's doing the right thing; must have reassurance, a committee decision, before he can throw himself wholeheartedly into giving.

With flippers: Has everything it takes to be giving and loving, but it's usually with a purpose. This person is driven to achieve something and to make generous gestures count. Acts with flair and courage; others are probably made to feel like they've been given to. It's all part of the plan.

p

Some people are self-starters. They generate their own positive attitude, always expecting the best from every situation. Others can never believe that things will turn out okay. They expect the worst from any situation and rely on friends and family to give their confidence a kick-start. The *p* tells us who is who.

a positive attitude

No doubt about it, thoughts are powerful things. Every idea we conceive, each dream we dream, is a building block toward the future. And whether the type of structure we assemble is weak and temporary or sturdy enough to become a lifelong triumph is entirely up to us. We are who we are and what we are and where we are right now because, somewhere down the line, *we decided to be*. No one else can be held accountable. In the words of William Henley,

> It matters not how strait the gate,
> How charged with punishments the scroll,
> I am the master of my fate:
> I am the captain of my soul.

You too are the master of your fate, and it is the quality of your thoughts, tallied on a daily basis, that in the end will determine whether your stay on this planet is a happy, profitable one or littered with disappointment and heartache. Whatever way you expect life to turn out, it generally rises to meet your expectations. So if you're the sort of person who constantly looks for the downside, the dark lining inside every silver cloud, if you believe that people are sneaky and unreliable, or that they're not going to like you, or that whatever you try to do it's sure to turn out for the worst, then that's exactly how it will turn out. Your word is law. Your thoughts are powerful enough to draw the reality toward you. So why waste all that energy fearing the worst when the same amount of energy, fueling a positive outlook, could make all the difference?

Pessimism makes no sense. It stokes up a thousand doubts and fears that eat away at your confidence. "In the long run," said Daniel Reardon, "the pessimist may be proved to be right, but the optimist has a better time on the trip." Surely it makes more sense, then, to approach life in a spirit of joyful anticipation, secretly relying on the universe to come up trumps, knowing all will be well. Expect the best, and the best is what you'll get.

The most important thing is to be positive.
That's my blood group, you know—B-Positive.
—Jeremy Hanley

p

Check out the length of the stem and whether the "nose" on the *p* rises up or droops down. This is a difficult one to measure, but usually the more rounded and buoyant the *p* is, then the more optimistic the writer will be. If it looks miserable, that probably reflects his attitude toward life right now.

Upright, sturdy: Confident and expectant, with a positive attitude, enough to get him through the difficult times. Expects things to turn out okay. Tends to look on the bright side. Good to have around. A positive vibe lifts everyone's spirits and makes the impossible seem possible. Could teach the rest of us a lesson or two.

Upright, with flippers: Positive attitude. Demands recognition and good service and expects others to live up to their promise. If they do, the writer's attitude will be friendly and agreeable. If they don't, it causes frustration and annoyance. Won't like wasting time on foolish or miserable folk, but his outlook is influenced by other people's moods.

Drooping nose: Glum, despondent and pessimistic about the outcome of current situations. Care-worn and fearful. Sees only dark skies, convinced there is worse to come. Needs help from friends to bolster confidence and reassess problems. Things are never as bad as they seem. Negative attitude must change, though, before circumstances will.

High stem: Judges his actions by standards and principles set by parents or teachers. Feels he must live up to them. Has been taught to be resilient and never give up. Tenacious and dutiful. Can be relied on to keep smiling even during the toughest times. Not easily defeated. Excellent leadership qualities if applied correctly.

Loose, disjointed: Always ready to listen to other people's opinions—perhaps *too* ready, in fact. Easily caught up in fascinating but irrelevant side issues. May drift with the popular current rather than sticking with what he knows. Some might call him easily led; he considers himself easygoing.

Long thread: Struggling to keep it all together. Much effort goes into appearing positive, but is this positivity genuine? Confidence may be shaky. Half of this person wants to be left alone to handle situations in his own way, while the other half knows he needs the cooperation of those around him. Tricky.

Plunging stem: At first glance, this person may not appear too optimistic, but his attitudes are drawn from rich experience and inner knowing. He has plenty to offer with plenty left in reserve. A gentle or unassuming exterior hides a sturdier interior. Don't be deceived.

Flyaway: Won't take responsibility for his own moods or outlook on life. He's short on real contentment. Optimism is external, with no personal foundation. Too busy weighing up his relationships with others, comparing his performance with theirs, to be wholly effective and make all the right moves.

Looped stem: Actions, hopes and attitudes are all drawn from the writer's personal experience and lessons learned over the years. He has strong gut feelings about what should be done and what might happen as a consequence of his decisions. Parental input shaped his approach to life's little problems.

Curled over: He may be optimistic, but that doesn't stop his heart from missing a beat in times of trouble. Faith is not so blind that he doesn't raise the question, "What will happen to me if everything goes wrong?" Under the cool exterior the blood pressure is rising and serious questions are being asked.

Since his arrival last summer, he's taken on two key roles in the production of the programme. He's been a terrific studio producer and is looking ahead to a project on the summer in India.

This woman has a lot on her mind. The handwriting slopes downward, showing that she is coping with many pressures at present and feeling gloomy about her ability to handle it all. This is backed up by her tight, almost crushed p's, proving that she is less than optimistic about the future.

q The ability to handle criticism—that's what the letter *q* is really all about. Will the writer crumple like damp tissue in the face of opposition or stand up for himself and fight his corner? Is he eager to put his ideas across or too sensitive, fearful and shy?

resilience

These are tough, demanding times. So it pays to build up a strong outer shell of resilience to protect yourself from criticism, rejection or any other form of attack you might encounter along your road to personal fulfillment. Sounds like a hard job, but luckily, the universe is on your side in this.

Each new challenge you face in life presents you with a straight choice: fight or flight. In other words, rise to the occasion, speak your mind, tackle any problem head-on or run away and leave someone else to deal with it. No prizes for guessing which approach carries the biggest rewards! The first boosts your self-esteem, giving you the spirit and stamina to fight another day, while the other weakens it, leaving you altogether less sure and feeling less able to cope next time around.

Frail, defensive types are generally too thin-skinned to succeed. Their egos are delicate; they bruise too easily. Time and again, they sabotage their chances of making it by taking everything too personally, wasting valuable energy worrying over where the next attack might be coming from. If you accept that there's plenty to be gained by speaking out and expressing your ideas clearly, then you must also accept that the more outspoken you are in support of your aims and beliefs, the more likely you are to be criticized for them. That's the price you pay for trying. By raising the stakes, you also increase the odds of being slapped down. Not everyone is going to like you, and not everyone is going to like what you have to say. So you must expect conflict occasionally. Expect to be misunderstood and expect to defend your opinions passionately before those who don't share your point of view.

Work at being resilient. Build up your inner strength so that, no matter how many knocks you take along the way, you always remain unshaken and ready to bounce back for the next round.

To escape criticism, do nothing,
say nothing, be nothing.
—Elbert Hubbard

---

q

Check out the slant of the *q*. Which way does it lean? A left slant usually belongs to someone who expresses ideas openly, squares up to any opposition and says what must be said. A right-hand slant often indicates a fear of rejection. This person won't enter into arguments because he fears he might lose.

Upright, sturdy: Talks and listens in equal measure. Can take reasonable criticism without overreacting or feeling hurt. May not be the most aggressive negotiator: Prefers to be slow and sincere, but expects to be heard. Not an open book; will keep some plans secret, presenting them later when the time is right. The gentle approach pays dividends.

Small head, tail flicked away: Has ideas, but probably doesn't think you'll understand them. Keeps them well out of reach until he feels the time is right. Could become defensive if criticized and possibly say things to upset others. If his opinions don't receive the right reception, he would rather walk away than risk outright humiliation.

Left slant: Eager to communicate ideas and make proposals. Wants to be heard. May even be aggressive in his approach if he believes passionately in what he's saying. Confronts issues squarely, but in his own "special way." Not the type to get trampled in the rush. Most likely doesn't know the meaning of the word no.

Right slant: Signs of fear. Reluctant to show strength, prefers to withdraw and fight another day. Could be thrown off balance completely by aggressive tactics. Won't be too forthright in case he is wrong and others spot the flaws. Lacks the confidence to really win through. Time to sign up for that assertiveness course.

Large head, short stem: Sensitive to criticism. Seeks acceptance and approval and takes rejection badly. Gets caught up in petty arguments almost before he can stop himself. Often wounded by thoughtless words and actions; may take offense where no offense was meant.

Flyaway tail: Keeps ideas safely hidden until the time is right. Doesn't trust others with them. Likes to deal with everything himself in his own way. Resourceful, with many tricks up his sleeve. An independent thinker with a plan for every occasion.

Right slant with flyaway tail: Anxious to protect his own interests at all costs. Says, "There's no way I'm telling you my plans if you're going to criticize them or steal them from me." Either a bit of a wimp or, more likely, he's genuinely afraid that others will run off with his best ideas and claim them as their own.

Small, tight, sharp: Self-protective, tough and probably quite shrewd, too. A strategist who knows his own mind and is not afraid to voice his opinion. If others disagree, that's their problem. He says, "Don't mess with the best," and means it!

Small, delicate, round: Afraid of being attacked and proved wrong. Doesn't like the finger of blame to point directly at him. Recoils at the first sign of disagreement. Tender, hurtable and even slightly weak at times. Would like to be stronger and come out fighting, but doesn't really have the confidence.

Creeping ivy tail: Wears his heart on his sleeve. May not be so sure of his ideas but always hopes they'll be accepted. Criticism strikes deep, however. He is sincere and uncynical and therefore open to exploitation. Others need to recognize a genuine spirit and give him space. Above all, be kind.

Hooded: Determined to win points without making concessions. Enjoys standing his ground, hides behind severe or tough temperament. Objections are brushed aside, obstacles met head-on. This person feels he is constantly fighting a battle, but is it one of his own making? Could afford to bend a little sometimes; if so, just watch the difference.

r

The letter *r* is a useful device if you want to know how aware a person is of what is going on around him. Does he have a wider interest in other people's affairs and keep his ear to the ground? Or is he the type who focuses only on the job at hand, leaving others to get on with their own lives?

dedication

Dedication is really just another form of giving. It means devoting yourself lovingly to a task for its own sake and completing it to the highest possible standard, not because you have to but because there is real joy and satisfaction to be found in a job well done. A dedicated gardener, for instance, has a simple yet profound love of nature. He receives untold pleasure from nurturing his flowers and trees and watching them grow from season to season. Any money he receives for his efforts is almost incidental.

To be dedicated means striving always for higher standards, making sure no job is left half done and nothing shoddy gets through the net. It also means being reliable. How often have you promised faithfully to do something for someone and really meant it at the time, but then, later on, changed your mind and tried to wriggle out of the commitment? We've all done this sort of thing. Made promises and welched on them, fixed appointments and turned up late or sometimes not at all, undertaken to return a difficult phone call and then deliberately misplaced the number. But this isn't dedication. If we fail to honor our commitments to others, if we let them down without a second thought and keep doing it, we earn a reputation for being unreliable. In the end, people lose faith in us. When we let them down, we're really letting ourselves down.

So if you promise to do something, do it, whatever the cost and however long it takes. Make a name for yourself as someone who not only says he'll do something, but goes right ahead and does it. Dedicate yourself to being the best you can be at all times. Like the gardener, put in your best effort for its own sake, because it feels like the right thing to do, not because of what might be in it for you. Once you've got the reliability habit, stick to it and watch it pay dividends.

Easy is right. Begin right and you are easy.
Continue easy and you are right!
—Chuang Tsu

---

r

Average: Alert, and aware of what is going on. Won't miss much. This person responds well to others and likes to know how they're doing. Tries to balance natural curiosity and the urge to communicate with a dedication to duty. Too much chat with others could mean lower performance. Should guard against mixing work and pleasure.

Vertical: Won't go in search of information; prefers to wait for the juicy details to come to him. Has an antenna, like a sixth sense, that picks up data from many sources. Sits, watches, listens, absorbs. Brilliant at knowing what's going on but without always showing it. Mind split in two: one half on the job, the other picking up vibes.

Stooped: Highly conscientious. May have a plodding approach to work, slow but dedicated. Just gets on with it. Not always interested in office gossip or other people's lives—not if they get in the way of the job at hand, anyway. Prefers to keep going and finish what he sets out to do, if possible without interruption.

Leaning out: A little too eager to find out what's going on. Other things must wait. His parents may have taught him that it's wrong to pry into other people's affairs, but what the hell? There's an unquenchable curiosity here. Everything else gets put on the back burner. Strangely, he'll probably keep his own private affairs under wraps.

Sniffing the ground: Dogged, conscientious, unstoppable when he's on the case. His endless dedication makes him a pillar of the workplace, someone who keeps going and won't give up until he's spotted all the flaws, covered all the bases. You can run from him, but you can't hide.

High stem: High standards of behavior were set in childhood. This person was taught to stand apart and survey a scene from a distance rather than dive in too quickly. He can keep an eye on several situations at once. Occasionally, recklessness may win over duty, but it goes against the grain.

Crooked arm: Protects certain details with care. Can you ever be sure what's really going on behind that cool, dutiful facade? This writer is usually protecting something, so don't take everything he does or says at face value. There's more going on than meets the eye.

Stooped, with flipper: Don't go thinking that, just because his head's down and he looks busy he won't see what's going on. He will. Dedicated and alert, he'll pick up on details you missed. Not the sort to welcome interference when he's engrossed in some vital task. He thinks he's in control.

Needle-sharp: Feels compelled to do whatever needs doing, and will push on, probably against all the odds, keeping to the point, staying on course. Able to spot the details that matter and discard anything irrelevant. There is a force driving him on, a sense of duty or honor that must be satisfied.

Angular: Once this person's mind is on the job he's not easily distracted. Wants answers and results and he's not moving 'til he gets 'em. Uses mechanical and probably methodical actions, and may lack finesse somehow. The type who makes a stand and sticks with it until he's ready to move on.

Raised whip: Haggles over matters of principle, cites rules and reasons. Always making valuable suggestions, which he believes will cause the system to work more smoothly, and can't figure out why nobody listens. Believes he has the answers, if only people would pay attention.

Looped stem: Insecurities underlie the writer's interest in the world and other people. Nothing is simple, nothing as plain as it appears. Has reasons for holding back and not giving the job his best shot. May be jealous of others or harbor a secret fear that they will succeed where he has not.

Sharp, ornate: Caught in a two-way split. A battle rages constantly between the need to get things done and the personal doubts and fears lurking in his head. Should he stay or should he go? What is right and what is wrong? Others may be confused by his motivations, though it all works out in the end.

Even in a scribbled grocery list there's is no hiding the truth. See the word "litter" and the way the r reaches out to the right? This woman has her finger on the pulse. That r works overtime, like an antenna, picking up signals from every which way. Dedicated? Probably, but she's more likely to be chasing information and haggling over what she discovers than really getting on with the job at hand.

S

The s can be a very dynamic letter. It shows whether the writer is driven by a deep desire to achieve his aims and push his plans through to fruition or if he hesitates and dithers too much and never really gets his ideas off the ground.

determination

Determination is the engine that powers success. Without it, nothing worthwhile can be achieved. It is not enough merely to have a goal. It is not even enough to take direct action toward achieving that goal. What really matters in the end is *follow-through*, whether you have the stamina and the staying power to persevere until you make that goal a glorious reality.

We build our successes the same way we build a house—from the ground up, laying brick upon brick, stone upon stone, until the job is done and the structure complete. And, as with a house, if you don't have the commitment to keep going and finish the job, or you quit at the first sign of rain or when your back starts creaking from all the hard work, what's going to happen? You'll end up with no home, or at least a very unsatisfactory one with three very shaky walls and no roof! The answer always is to apply yourself, don't settle for half measures. Stick with it until you get where you want to be. Of course you need to be realistic, too. When the going gets rough and your path is strewn with obstacles, ask yourself: Is this the best way to go? Could there be an easier way around? After all, would you blast your way through a mountain if you could just as easily fly over the top?

Constantly fine-tune your plans to ensure you're on the right course, and if all the signs say you are, then keep going no matter what. If people think you're stubborn, fine, let them think it. If they accuse you of being blinkered or bull-headed, brush them aside with a cheerful "Sure, that's me!" and move on. Adversity is the litmus of faith, and only by continuing on in a spirit of total determination and self-belief do we achieve what we set out to do. So keep on keeping on. Let no one stand in your way. Do whatever you have to do and persevere until you reach your destination.

Perseverance is not a long race,
it is many short races one after another.
—Walter Elliot

S

> **Check out** which way the *s* is leaning and whether there are loops on it. A forward slant usually indicates determination, whereas a backward slant belongs to a more impulsive person, someone who acts first and thinks later. A top loop means stubbornness, a bottom loop directness.

Relaxed, rounded: Open, easygoing. Listens intellligently, then takes positive action. Willing to accept new information and shape actions accordingly. Swims with the tide, never too slow, never too hasty. Game, adventurous and determined, but only in the right circumstances. Chooses his moment to make an impact.

Pert, upright: Ready for anything. Inner strength means this person is willing to roll up his sleeves and get down to the task at hand, doing whatever it takes to make it a success. An eager participant. There is a strong spirit here, a strength of will, which, if coupled with a single purpose, could produce amazingly positive results.

Pert, but rounded: Ready for anything—but in a relaxed way. Willing to let events unfold before diving in. Likes to make an impact, but is more circumspect than others and happy to adopt a gentler approach. Jobs will get done, but in this person's own way and when the time is right, not before. Don't rush him.

Top loop: Stubborn, fixed in his ways. Has a plan set firmly in mind and won't wish to deviate from it. It makes no difference that others disagree or throw obstacles in his way, he will simply step over them and move on. Spirited, obstinate, not easily persuaded to change course. Stand back and watch this person go!

Straight and thin: A driven personality perhaps, but rather characterless, too. His methods tend to work, but are unadventurous on the whole. Presents an image of drifting forward with determination but without detailing the exact nature of his plans.

Sharp, with inner loop: Any doubts, reservations or fears are kept out of sight behind a stubborn front. The writer could be a contender if he wanted to be, but succeeds more by default than direct participation. Much is going on under the surface. Tough, resilient, hard to knock back.

With flipper: Strong, demanding. Ready to pull others into line if they break the rules. If you've got an excuse, this person doesn't want to hear it. Just do what you said you would do, then move out of the way. Knows his rights and expects you to know—and respect—them, too.

Looped behind: Resourceful, willing to press on whatever the cost. This person never gives up. He sees possible ways forward where others see only blockages, and always has something up his sleeve. Knock him back and he'll find another way through. Unstoppable when his mind is set.

Looped across: Direct, to the point, and not afraid to hear the word _no._ In fact, rejection only fires his spirit. "If you don't ask, you don't get." So he keeps on asking until someone gives him what he wants. He may speak out of turn occasionally and regret it, but that's just part of the game.

Rounded: A general eagerness to move on and see what's around the next corner is softened by his "go with the flow" attitude. This person knows you can only move so fast and get just so much done in one day. May be held back by present responsibilities, but these are under control.

Rounded with upward curl: The gentler, more philosophical side of the writer's nature is being sorely tested. In an effort to sort matters out and be all things to all people, he feels he is losing ground, asking for favors without knowing if he'll get them. Not the best state to be in!

Figure of eight: Itching to make a move and get things done. Like a loaded spring, could uncoil at any moment. May act impetuously when he knows he should sit back and go with the flow, but patience is not in his makeup—at least not when there is something he is desperate to achieve.

Partial cross loop: This person's needs and goals don't get expressed too well. He knows what he wants and he *intends* to express it fully, but then, at the last minute, he holds back. When the chips are down he could lose out by not making his intentions clear.

Leaning back: Raring to go. While others are asking questions, playing it safe, this person is getting things done. A streak of good sense lies behind his actions, but there is conflict, too. His head is saying one thing while his heart says another. Which will win?

Blocked: Knows his own mind and what he wants to achieve. He's not interested in contrary viewpoints or in the arguments of those who try to stand in his way. This person barges on through like a bull at a gate until he gets his way. Determined—and how!

Sharpened: Pursues goals fiercely. Determined, intense, not easily thrown off course or distracted. Knows what he wants and plans to get it. Those who stand in his way are either beaten into submission or ignored as he marches on toward his chosen destination. Not to be tangled with.

Long tail in back: Expects results. There are many considerations to be taken into account in any decision he makes. Nothing is simple and nothing is too clear. He knows what he wants but there is so much to coordinate and he could miss the bigger picture by fussing over details.

t

The *t*'s job is to reflect the writer's honesty and integrity—what he really feels in his heart rather than what his actions may show on the surface. It tells you whether or not this person is in touch with his emotions, whether he is passionate and loving and whether his motives are genuine and can be trusted.

honesty, sincerity, love and passion

People want to trust us and to believe in us. They need to know that we'll be fair in our dealings with them and that the emotions we show are genuine and sincere. This spirit of integrity is called "being true," and it forms the cement in all meaningful human relationships.

Young children offer us the clearest understanding of what it means to be true. If you have kids of your own, then you'll know already how painfully honest and sincere they can be. A child's logic says; "If something is funny and I want to laugh and roll around on the floor, that's exactly what I'm gonna do" and "You know when I hurt myself? Well, I won't stifle that emotion, no sir—I'm gonna cry, and I'm gonna keep on crying until the pain goes away." That's how it is with kids, all wonderfully obvious and straightforward. They're just raw material: loving, spontaneous, experimental, enthusiastic—all the things humans were intended to be—and they do it without even trying.

Unfortunately, as we grow older, everything that was once so simple suddenly becomes very complicated. Often, instead of making us kinder and more sincere and trusting, life teaches us to be harder and more guarded; we find that the sense of adventure we had when we were kids, all the exciting risks we took and the way we expressed ourselves so freely and honestly—are all gone, buried under a thick layer of caution and inhibition. But that inner child is never lost. He or she is still there, sheltering in our heart, waiting to be rediscovered. All it takes is the will to release it, coupled with a readiness to explore once more the kind of person we are inside. Where our inner child is, that's where our character and our life-purpose are also. By discovering one we uncover the others. Suddenly, we realize that there is more to who we are than what we have become.

———————

The love we give away is the only love we keep.
—Elbert Hubbard

———————

t

Check out where the crossbar of the *t* strikes across the stem. Through the middle—fine: the writer is in touch with his heart. Too high, he prefers reason and logic to deeper emotions, and thinks too much. On the other hand, if the crossbar doesn't cross the stem at all, he may be insincere and detached from his feelings.

Bar crosses middle: On the whole, a genuine person who means what he says and says what he means. It may not always be the truth, but *he* believes it. Feelings run deep. Emotions are displayed openly. Likely to be trustworthy, passionate when aroused, and have a caring nature that makes him worth knowing.

Supported at the back: This person has a set pattern of behavior and beliefs, which shapes his view of the world. Childhood conditioning has left a lasting impression. Feelings and opinions are genuine and firm but have been molded by years of experience and "training." Believes he knows what's right and what could be done to make things better.

High crossbar: A thinker. Prefers logic, ideas, a frank exchange of views, to displays of emotion. May be afraid of showing feelings, or uncomfortable with their power. Likes to stay within known boundaries. Sees emotions as illogical, not easily contained. Secretly seeking release but finds it hard to go beyond limitations.

Extended crossbar: Big on feelings, big on communication of beliefs. Likes to tell people what to do, the correct way to approach things. Believes he's right at all times and believes others should listen and follow his lead. Awkward if contradicted. Not easy to argue with. Don't pick a fight with him. If you do, expect trouble.

Looped stem: Wrestling with issues of personal value. Self-questioning and doubt contribute to this person's performance but could get in the way of expressing true feelings openly. Confused about own capabilities and needs. Looking for reassurance.

Low crossbar: Confuses love with sex. Much thought goes into the physical side of relationships rather than into communicating deeper feelings. A certain amount of cunning may underlie his actions too at times. He wants only one thing!

Detached crossbar: Does whatever has to be done to get results. Entrenched behavior patterns lead him to follow procedure and expect others to do the same. Motivations go unquestioned. Not in touch with his feelings on some level. Watch out for a possible ruthless streak, too.

Crossbar to left of stem: Has been through a lot and survived. Now he's trying to put the past behind him and move on. Won't fall for the same tricks a second time. Pain, buried deep inside, fuels current actions. Trying to erase hurtful memories, but it's not easy.

Tiny crossbar: Small-time emotions. Not very expressive or demonstrative. Cool, controlled, muted. Many powerful feelings are kept locked up inside, but without generating much benefit. Low-key actions breed low-key reactions from others. Where's the passion, the heat, the enthusiasm?

Flying crossbar: Imaginative, idealistic, even slightly detached. Big on thoughts and ideas, perhaps with a dreamy, unreal view of love. Too lost in his own world ever to get totally lost in yours. Take him for what he is or not at all.

Upward slope on crossbar: Has firm beliefs and is proud of them. Argumentative when challenged. Tends to back his own judgment and is difficult to convince if his mind is made up. Friends find him unwilling to listen to reason. He believes he has the answers, if only other people would give him credit.

Downward slope on crossbar: Listens to others and shares their opinions and feelings. Believes problems can be worked out sensibly and easily if everyone stays calm. Not a strong performer in heated arguments. May give in to please others or for peace of mind.

Double-cross: Exactly what it says. Two crossbars usually indicate deceit: the sign of a two-timer, someone who covers his tracks as he goes. Take care before passing judgment, but watch out for double standards, divided loyalties, or a person who enjoys living dangerously.

Coat hook: Probably fairly humble, decent and trustworthy. Often feels small and unworthy when pitched alongside others. Fears rejection or making too much of an impact, in case there are repercussions. Underneath, he's reaching out to be loved. Alas, could get trampled in the rush.

Reverse coat hook: Who is that masked stranger? Personal details are kept locked away until the writer feels ready to reveal his innermost secrets—which may be never. Some issues are being deliberately overlooked or hidden from view. He feels it would be better if you simply didn't know.

Reverse coat hook, with loop: This person feels that certain emotional issues should not be discussed or even addressed. We all have them, he thinks, so why burden other people with my problems? Keep them under wraps and you keep them out of harm's way, that's the logic here.

Back and across: Expect a certain amount of style and grace. Lots of fun, too. Although this outer facade may hide a determined, clever and, in some cases, quite prickly character. Don't be fooled—you're dealing with a skilled social operator here, however much he tries to conceal it.

Back support plus back and cross: Caught up in a tangle of emotions. Can be entertaining and lively and seem carefree, but he is struggling to escape childhood conditioning and the wishes of parents and others that were imposed upon him when he was young. Still searching for his own path.

Double t, firmly crossed: What you see is what you get. This person is straightforward and means exactly what he says. Transparent motives are translated into clear, unmistakable actions. Coordinated and resolute, he generally stays true to his beliefs and principles.

Small left t, tall right t: The writer appears more confident and "together" than he really feels. Inside, he is modest, humble and unsure of who he really is and what he wants. This person is caught up on a treadmill that he feels unable to stop. Needs to catch his breath and consider options.

Left-hand cross only: Deep feelings and beliefs often go unexpressed or else they come out the wrong way. This person hasn't got the knack of putting his thoughts into words, so his motives may be misunderstood. Unless he communicates more clearly, how can others ever see his point of view?

Way too tall: Has a high opinion of himself, which may not be justified. He is unaware of many of his own limitations. His sense of a boundless horizon matched with great personal expectations could lead to disappointment or frustration as the years go by if he doesn't get a grip on reality soon.

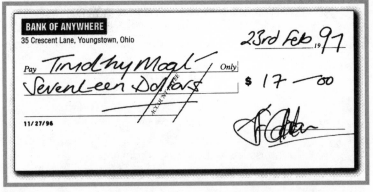

Note how this man doesn't cross the t's on his check, indicating a certain amount of insincerity. He has lost touch with his emotions or his conscience on some level. That's not to say he's dishonest, but a t with a flying crossbar like this is often a strong indicator that a person will do whatever has to be done. May be ruthless, self-serving, or, in extreme cases, dishonorable. Take extra care, just in case.

u

the lone rider

Socializing, done in moderation, is an important part of life. It's good to party, to escape from reality now and then and go a little crazy. But equally as important is the time we spend alone.

"Alone time" is a period of renewal. Think of it as a gift to yourself, a few hours each week when you shut off the TV, unplug the phone and slowly bring mind and body into a state of composed stillness, away from the stresses and hassle of the world outside. Or you might escape to a favorite location, somewhere peaceful and quiet. Some of our most penetrating thoughts come to us when we're ambling through a forest, say, or sitting on rocks gazing out at the ocean, or even when we're just lying down in a steaming hot aromatic bath—anyplace where we have time on our hands and the space to let our mind open up and breathe.

Quiet relaxation heightens your powers of awareness, creating the right environment for clear communication with your higher self. Slowly, valuable insights and extraordinary inspirations filter down to you from the intuitive side of the brain, as you begin trading ideas with the universe. It's like logging on to the spiritual Internet! Here, in this magical moment, is when you will hear your inner voice speaking to you, giving you clear ideas and instructions for living. What is normally a whisper lost in the bang and crash of everyday life becomes a big, booming voice of reassurance as you drift in stillness, alone with your thoughts.

The more we cultivate aloneness and build it into our routine, the better we become at addressing our life issues and deciding what the next step on our spiritual journey should be. A period spent in quiet contemplation gives us all the nourishment and energy we need to face up to our problems and handle them with assurance, wisdom and resilience.

What fools call loneliness,
wise men know as solitude.
—Ching Chow

---

u

Check out whether the *u* is standing alone or is connected to the letters on either side of it. A connected *u* belongs to a sociable person, while a disconnected one means the writer enjoys his own company and does not need to be surrounded by crowds of people all the time.

Connected: Likes to have fun with others. Gets pleasure from meeting and greeting, mixing and fixing. Open to all kinds of social experience. Variety is important. No reasonable offer ever refused. Feels comfortable in a crowd. In fact, group activities are preferable to solitary pursuits. A party animal and a bit of a social climber, too.

Disconnected: The stand-alone type. Enjoys time spent reading, meditating, listening to music, pursuing a hobby or chatting with a close friend. There may be occasions when he wants other people around and can't get enough of the social scene. But not always. Sometimes, it's got to be peace and quiet and solitude. Give him space.

Tight: Lack of room inside the *u* indicates narrowness of tastes. This person likes what he likes but nothing more. Tame, unadventurous, slow to commit to anything that takes him outside his comfort zone. Keeps enthusiasms under wraps and prefers a small number of close friends and familiar faces to big crowds. This person is an acquired taste.

Tiny, fragile: Low-key personality seeking low-key entertainment. Never goes too far; seldom, if ever, embarrassingly loud. Socializes with others, but tries to stay within a particular group. May want to break out of straitjacket and occasionally does just that. Rare, though. Won't feel comfortable alongside high-octane personalities.

Looped: This person enjoys complex relations with others, although "enjoys" may not be the right word. Nothing is ever straightforward. Swirling emotional undercurrents mean nobody is sure what to expect or where they stand. Confusion could be averted with a bit of straight talking.

Stretched flat: Sociable, but easily pleased. Whatever happens, wherever you go, is just fine for this person. Not the least bit demanding or difficult, usually. Likes others to think he's easygoing but in the end he may just seem vague or indecisive.

Curled in: Too choosy. Invitations are turned down, parties snubbed, people left out in the cold. There are barriers here. He may have a bored streak or just feel threatened by too much action and like to keep the world at bay. Feels he's fine as he is; anything more would be unwelcome.

V

This is often a good way to discover how experienced the writer is in bed. The letter *v* shows us whether he is naïve and still learning, or has an expansive and open attitude to sex based on years of practice. The *v* can even reveal whether or not this person is in the mood for sex *today*.

sexual performance

Pick up any glossy magazine these days and the subject of sex is usually right there, glaring back out at you. Who's doing it to whom and how often? Is such-and-such a celebrity good in bed? Is Mr. X really doing *that* to Miss Y behind closed doors? We've become obsessed with the subject.

But what does "good in bed" mean, anyway? In fact, there's no such thing. It's a myth. What seems good to me might seem fumbling and incompetent to someone else. We often forget it, but sex is an instinctive drive, not something we need to be taught! There's nothing mystical or dangerous or threatening about it, nothing to get hung up about. Sure, good technique can always be learned—there are thousands of interesting ways to refine the experience and make it even better for both partners—but everything you need to know, all the basics for pleasure and fulfillment, are already programmed in, naturally. In fact, worrying about our performance—whether we're doing it right and living up to our partner's expectations—can prevent us from doing it at all. What really matters is that we relax into the experience and enjoy it, using lovemaking as a physical expression of our feelings for the other person, not as some kind of points-scoring exercise intended to dazzle and impress our partner.

The secret of expansive sex is to go with whatever feels right in the moment. To be oneself and always be spontaneous and honest in one's affections. In the end, the only right way is your own way. If you're happy and your partner's happy, then you're "good in bed"—that's all there is to it.

Personally, I know nothing about sex, because I've always been married.
—Zsa Zsa Gabor

V

Check out the spread of the arms on the *v*. If they're wide and embracing, the writer has quite an appetite for good sex and the right experience to back it up. The narrower and tighter those arms become, the more inhibited he is likely to be—maybe generally, or maybe it's just today. If a *v* is tight, better face it: He's just not in the mood.

Good spread: Frank and expansive view of sex. Rules nothing in and nothing out. Game for whatever happens. He knows what he likes and goes all out to get it. Gives and receives love warmly. If the *v* is not connected to the letters on either side, he probably enjoys one-night stands and indulges in sex for its own sake.

Tight: A little inhibited—maybe not always, but certainly at the moment. Could have a low sex drive. Generally not the type to indulge in weird or adventurous activities. Scared of letting go, of being unconventional and opening up to the wider experience. Inhibitions may be rooted in childhood, when sex was given a bad label.

High right arm: Whether the *v* is broad or tight, a high right means the writer will go so far but no farther. Expect a challenge. This person needs coaxing and persuasion; wants to know his partner is genuine and doing it for all the right reasons. Self-protective, slightly fearful of being hurt. Look, but don't touch!

With flippers: Flippers off the top of a *v* reveal whether this person does the asking or waits to be asked. A *left* flipper means he makes the first approach and leads his partner toward the bedroom. A *right* flipper says, "Come and get me!" Find the right formula—romance, candlelight, music—then just watch him go!

Pulled back: Wants to be adventurous, but other factors get in the way of a good time. Thinks: Maybe others won't approve or What would my parents say if they found out? Either a little inhibited or just reluctant to let go completely and follow his natural urges.

Rooted left: Brings quite an understanding and attitude to sex, but also a set of beliefs and limits. His approach as an adult will depend on his parents' approach to sex when he was growing up. Ready and willing perhaps, but not as much as he should be.

Rooted right: Seductive and alluring. Knows a whole range of tricks that have been proved to work and is not scared of using them if it means he gets what he wants. Experience has taught him what works and what doesn't, and he plays the game for all it's worth.

Closed: May have been hurt once too often in the past in relationships, or is too scared to try. This person is nurturing a guarded, self-defeating attitude, which causes him to hold back when he should be reaching out. Needs to look inward and ask, What am I really scared of?

Pulled both ways: This writer is involved in an emotional struggle, probably by choice. He uses various tricks to win over possible partners and definitely enjoys the thrill of the chase—the more drama the better. Wants to feel wanted but likes playing hard to get.

Rounded: This person is either young and naïve or simply hanging on to the attitudes of youth for too long. He promises playful, innocent, gentle fun but his technique may be lacking in sophistication or daring. Has a lot to learn.

Tiny: Emotions are being held in. Someone with a limited sexual range and an inability to express true feelings openly. Possibly a cold fish, difficult to arouse. Once you have earned his trust the ice may thaw, revealing warmth and passion beneath. Be patient.

Large, wide open: Anything goes. Sex is indulged in for reasons of personal endorsement. Making love compensates for deep insecurity. What seems like a healthy or even voracious appetite for physical action may just be an invitation to say, "Baby, you were wonderful!"

Looped: Worries and self-doubt are attached to sexual activity. Can't open up fully because of a backlog of emotional baggage, which needs clearing out for good. May feel deprived or limited by personal fears or reservations. A new commitment to life and enjoyment is called for.

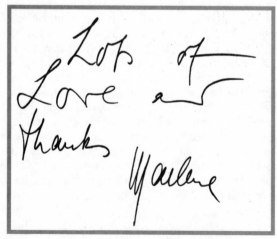

The bold, vibrant handwriting of screen goddess **Marlene Dietrich**. *Her v, with flippers on either side, shows she had a strong desire to flirt with men and draw them toward her, especially for support and reassurance. But there was an inner struggle. When she felt pain she wanted her men to know she was suffering. I'm sure she rather enjoyed a bit of drama!*

W

A handy device for measuring enthusiasm and what kind of energy lies behind the writer's actions. From the *w* we can tell whether he is excitable or laid back, easily impressed or quite discerning. It also tells us in certain cases whether this person has what it takes to be a winner.

enthusiasm

Within each one of us there stirs a passion, for a sport, maybe, for fishing, cooking, astronomy, stamps—it could be anything. We don't know why, there's no explaining it, but we're drawn to this subject like a magnet. Nothing else makes us as happy or fires our imagination in quite the same way. If only we could engage in this pursuit all day every day, we'd truly be in heaven!

Yet how many people, when it comes to choosing an occupation, completely overlook their passions, turning their back on the kind of work that would really set their juices flowing in favor of a job that's mundane and soul-destroying and to which they admit they're totally unsuited? "Still, it pays the bills," they say, and shrug wearily. Years later, of course, they realize that this money-first attitude was a mistake, by which time it's often too late; all they're left with are dreams of what might have been, if only . . .

Where your enthusiasm is, that's where you heart will be also. So live your passions for all they're worth, set them to work for you. Don't chicken out by making excuses: "I'm too old." "I don't have the right education." "I can't afford to take a big risk, I've got a family to support." These are important considerations, to be sure, but they're not the *only* considerations. Don't allow your decisions to be governed by self-doubt, especially in matters as crucial to personal happiness as your career; instead, indulge those enthusiasms. Fortune really does favor the brave, you know, just as surely as it turns its back on the apathetic, the cynical and the indifferent. The moment we back our talents with courage and committed action, we become bold and unstoppable. However distant our dreams once seemed, they're now, maybe for the first time, within our grasp. Your passions point the way to your destiny, so don't fight them—give in.

Every man has his own destiny;
the only imperative is to follow it,
to accept it, no matter where it leads him.
—Henry Miller

Check out the way the two hoops of the *w* hang together. Are they even and strong, revealing an enthusiastic nature? Or weak and straggly, meaning that the writer is easily excited and wastes his energy? If so, he may just waste his life, too—chasing rainbows, forever falling short of his dreams.

Sturdy, bold, both sides equal: Hallmark of a real enthusiast. Choosy about what he does. Won't waste time backing just any old fad. Needs to know his efforts will produce results. When interest is aroused, he'll be a great supporter, positive and encouraging. Carries others along on a tide of excitement.

Side-bars too high: Excited by anything and everything. Enthusiasm is way out of proportion to the subject. Sees potential in ideas where others can't, but may not act sensibly. Too busy looking for the pleasure element. Could be wasting valuable time and energy, but says, "Hey, who cares, so long as we're having fun?"

Sturdy, but sharp: Controlled. Enthuses genuinely but won't waste effort. Wants everything to be well organized. Coordination of resources is important. Finds chaotic situations disturbing and disorder frustrating. Better to keep a tight rein and ensure that everything runs smoothly.

Flyaway tail: Shares his enthusiasm. Likes to pitch in as part of a team effort. Grabs others' imagination, hoping to win them over. Good leadership spirit. (If this *w* is detached from other letters around it, then the writer likes others to be involved in his plans, but if they're not interested he'll happily continue alone.)

Arms curved inward: Sign of a winner. Wants to be the best. Not content just to win, though—must be *seen* to win. Otherwise why bother? Will put on a good show and do his best to make the grade but expects rewards for his effort—praise, attention, money, *something.*

Waving in the wind: Pretends to be cool about everything, but deep down he desperately wants others to participate. He endeavors to be tantalizing, but this may be inspired by low self-esteem. He's looking for acceptance, and could get huffy if ignored.

High middle: Impetuous. Gives whole heart to plans, though he may choose unwisely at times. Eager to be involved in situations and pursuits when wisdom might be telling him to hold back. If there are any problems, he'll shrug and say, "Hey, that's life," then move on to the next thing that catches his eye.

Tiny: Not visibly enthusiastic. Efforts are low-key and lack spirit. All activities have to be worthwhile and justified. He's a follower rather than a leader. If he rises to the top he'll need many followers to reassure him he's on the right course. Would benefit from showing passion.

Bulbous: Enthusiastic, but also defensive if criticized. Not the sort to give in without a fight. Likes others to approve of, and join in with, his plans. If they don't, he will feel quite hurt. Fragile ego needs gentle handling.

Stretched up: Selfish, fixed in his tastes and habits. Wants to do the things he wants to do and is therefore reluctant to give in to the wishes of others. Feels cramped or claustrophobic when others make too many demands on him. Let him go his own way.

X

> An *x* gives us a firm idea about the writer's sense of commitment. Is he faithful to his partner, for example? When he says, "You're the only one for me," does he really mean it? The *x* also reveals whether this person will be a loyal employee or the type who's forever searching for new opportunities.

Commitment

For some, the very idea of commitment is fraught with danger. They won't stick their neck out too far, afraid that if they do someone will step up and chop off their head. So they'd prefer to rent an apartment instead of committing to a loan and buying one; you hear they're engaged to be married, then, six months later, the wedding's off because they got cold feet. One sniff of responsibility and they're hunting for an escape route.

Then there are the indecisive ones. The way they see it, there's always the chance that something bigger and brighter and more thrilling may be right around the next corner, which of course they would miss if they committed to something else too soon. So they keep on searching, jumping from one enthusiasm to another, never stopping long enough in any one place to make a difference. Their entire life is spent chasing illusions, hunting restlessly for the Next Big Thing, which, when it arrives, rarely brings them joy or happiness anyway, simply because their eyes are already scanning the horizon for the Next Big Thing After That!

By committing to *anything*, you risk being disappointed—buying an expensive secondhand sports car just as they stop making spare parts for it; marrying Person A only to discover that Person B is better looking or hangs around with a more uptown crowd—but a spirit of commitment also brings its own rewards. You make a name for being trustworthy and reliable. Once your signature is on the dotted line, people know they can depend on you to go the distance and finish what you started. They see you mean business, that all your efforts, your emotions and energy are locked into this one single outcome. Make or break, you're *going* to produce a result. No one and nothing stands in the way of a person who knows what he wants and is determined enough and committed enough to go out there and get it.

Men are all alike in their promises,
it's only in their deeds that they differ.
—Molière

X

Check out the overall shape of the *x*. Ask, Does it look like a cross? If it does, the writer is committed both at work and within relationships and gives everything he's got to his partner and colleagues. Loops indicate a hidden agenda, someone who can't commit openly and freely.

Straight cross: A desire for commitment. Gives from the heart in the hope of receiving similar in return. Maybe a bit too optimistic and trusting, but he knows that unconditional giving generates plenty of goodwill and brings bountiful rewards. Open to being exploited or let down, but that's a small price to pay.

Looped: Has reservations. A lack of trust. Unwilling to go the whole way. Could be evasive if cornered. Take his promises with a pinch of salt. Many secret thoughts are going on behind paper-thin excuses. Confused about own needs, so is unable to meet the needs of others. Must reassess priorities, otherwise he could drift aimlessly.

Short down, long across: Possibly too reliant on partner. If needs aren't met he feels disillusioned, and also insecure when the reality of a relationship doesn't live up to his expectations. Seeking reassurance, backup, signs of stability. Would gain much from becoming more independent, making own decisions.

Back to back: Naïve, lovable, trusting. Commits too quickly, promises everything, gives unreservedly. Childlike approach to love. Has yet to grow up in some respects. Shields heart from reality, unable to face cynical truth. Deeply hurt by rejection. Affection could be intense and all-consuming. Let him down gently.

Bottom loop: Feels uncomfortable showing true feelings, simply because true feelings may be too dark or too intense. Old fears lurk beneath the surface and pent-up sexual and emotional energy seeks release. Unable to commit to another person until he has fully committed to himself.

Long down, short across: Always pushing to be the dominant partner. May be too keen to win, willing to do whatever it takes to make situations go his way. If the partner accepts this, then that's okay. Otherwise it could lead to daily power struggles and unhappiness.

Tiny: Simple commitment. May not have the imagination to be unfaithful. But don't play games with his affections, or he could wander. Be true to him and you will keep him; take liberties in love and he may well go looking for someone worthier of his attention.

Too big: Sensitive. Willing to give all and risk all, but not always sure to whom. Seeks satisfaction at all costs. Could invite trouble by being too keen. Searching for perfection but only finds compromise. The quest for personal endorsement could take its toll on his energies.

Tilted over: The writer's partner tends to have a great sense of commitment, or at least the partner makes more of a deal of it than the writer does. This person may feel trapped or hen-pecked, or constantly be made aware of his duties as one half of a loving relationship.

A man who needs no introduction: The long down-slash on **Richard Nixon**'s x *shows him to be almost too committed to his dealings. He was willing to go to any lengths to keep situations under control, and insisted on having the last word, whether he was right or wrong.*

y

The letter y covers a wide range of situations, all hung loosely on the idea of responsibility. If you want to know whether someone is reliable with money and pays his bills on time, whether he would rather delegate a task than do it himself, or if he can handle blame when he makes a mistake, then the y has all the answers.

taking responsibility

Human beings are perverse creatures. We're the most resourceful and robust species on the planet—built for action, positively *made* to live on our wits and tackle all kinds of challenges head-on—and yet most of us insist on running at well below full capacity, traveling Economy through life when, with the right amount of effort, we could be upgraded to First Class.

The only way we can discover what we're capable of is by testing ourselves, going beyond what we already know we can do and aspiring to something higher. We were born to achieve great things, to reach higher and travel farther than most of us ever allow ourselves, so you can afford to let your imagination roam freely on this one. Think big. Pull yourself out of the rut and dare to dream up a plan or adventure that would stretch you beyond the limits you have set for yourself. For some people, their first baby provides all the adventure they can handle. They find that steering their child through the minefield of those first few years is responsibility enough. Others get the same buzz from starting their own business, or running a soup kitchen for the homeless, or cutting up their credit cards and living within their income for the first time in years. It doesn't matter what you do, provided it drives you out of the groove of routine you've accepted as "normal" and into uncharted territory.

And if things go weird on you and don't work out quite the way you'd hoped, well, that's okay too. Don't sneak out the back door or go blaming other people for your mistakes; take responsibility for every new development, positive or negative, and accept it as just another step toward being a rounded, more knowledgeable and fulfilled individual. Know that, whatever hazards life may toss your way, you have everything you need to handle them. Everything and more.

The follies which a man regrets the most
in his life are those which he didn't commit
when he had the chance.
—Helen Rowland

y

Tail straight down: Cool under pressure. Accepts responsibility, handles problems with a sure hand. The buck stops here. Not the type to delegate without good reason. If there are deadlines, they will be met. Bills will usually be paid on time. Happy to stand up and be counted. Wow!

Looped tail: Action is calm, considered. Feels comfortable balancing own interests with outside duties. The bigger the loop, the greater the writer's preoccupation with his personal affairs. He thinks he can handle responsibility. Appearances may be deceptive, though. Unexpected events may wreck the cool façade.

Inward curl: May accept responsibility at first, but will no doubt run for cover the moment anything goes wrong. Does not enjoy being blamed *at all*! In fact, he can't believe anyone would dare accuse him of making mistakes. If the buck must stop here, expect a tantrum.

Over the shoulder: Willing to do everything possible to ensure a good result, but if there's a crisis he'll try to push the blame onto someone else. Not one to own up willingly to misdeeds if there is another way around. Why suffer the indignity of blame if another poor Joe or Joanne can take the flak instead? A bit cowardly, but shrewd.

Loop with flipper: Aware of responsibilities, deals with them in a matter-of-fact way. Puts other people first and his own affairs second. Believes in making a positive contribution and expects benefits in return. Likely to be a sound, committed member of the community.

Flyaway tail: Prone to delegating. If he seems to get more work done than others, that may be because he's giving others his work to do! Smart thinking. His dealings or actions may not always be entirely clearcut, so ask questions and make sure he is living up to his promises.

Pointed tail: Discerning. Able to handle many problems at once and keep several issues on the boil. Responsible, but busy. Likely to tell others what they should be doing and give them a sense of direction, but whether he knows what is right for himself is another matter.

Lurking tail: This person appears to be an open book, ready to welcome people and additional responsibilities, but various details are kept secret. He may also ignore relevant material rather than deal with it. Nothing ominous perhaps, but probe deeper just in case.

Big-lipped: Sharp, grumpy. Already feels like he's got too much to handle. Other people only make matters worse. Adopts a defensive attitude to keep others at a distance. Strong on telling folks what they can and cannot do, but that's just his way of maintaining some kind of control.

Bent over: Currently facing too much pressure—can't take the strain. Feels like he's going into battle every day, and is struggling to keep up. He may prefer to shrug off new responsibilities rather than face the extra hassle. Needs a long holiday.

Tail slopes down to the left: Dependable, smart and alert. Pays bills ahead of time and gets fairly uptight if financial affairs are muddled. Seeks reliability in return and expects others to be straight with him. Believes that by being "on the case" he can avert possible disaster in advance.

Tail slopes down to the right: There is too much work to be done and so little time to do it. He doesn't know where to start. Some tasks may never get completed because of a shortage of time. Dependable, and his heart's in the right place, but he needs to learn to delegate.

Curlaround tail: Fun, playful and slightly naughty, with many a trick up his sleeve. He'll seem perfectly serious and innocent on the surface, but behind the scenes you can bet he's up to no good. There is something devilish about his need to be one step ahead of the crowd.

Around and down: Probably the type who puts difficult tasks off until later, or keeps unfinished work hidden from those who might criticize him for not doing it. He fears that others will accuse him of letting the side down, and so backs away from this kind of confrontation.

Sharp and looped: Look out! He's up to something, though you may not be sure what. He often feels that outside forces are against him, so he is forced to rely on his tenacity and ingenuity to tackle the problem. He hates being trapped or oppressed, but it happens. A fighter.

Open-backed: Many onerous duties take up this person's time when in fact he'd rather be out there having fun. He feels that others should take their fair share of the burden by handling some of the boring stuff, but they won't, and he constantly gets stuck with it. Who said life was fair?

φ

Over and down: Not the type to tell you the whole story. He works according to his own agenda and could be quite selfish and demanding in fulfilling it. Wants others to fit in with his plans. If they don't, he'll squeeze them out and find someone who agrees to his agenda. Dynamic and infuriating.

y

Modest upward tail: Someone who takes life at his own pace. He deliberates, he considers, and only makes a move when he's ready. There may be signs of hesitation, but more likely you are dealing with a quiet, contemplative soul. Don't rush him. He'll come around soon enough.

7

Flat top: Preoccupied with business—*too* preoccupied, in fact, to the point of overlooking the basic pleasures of life. These go right over his head because his mind is elsewhere. He needs to refresh his memory about why he is alive and discover what he's missing.

Here we're looking at how critical the writer can be. How does he react to other people's views and ideas? The shape of the letter *z* tells us if he has a good sense of judgment and possesses the necessary wisdom to support what he's saying, or whether he opens his mouth and a whole load of junk falls out.

powers of judgment

One of the greatest threats to the success of any idea or plan is unsolicited advice—well-meaning words from parents, friends, partners and all the other kind folk who claim they have your best interests at heart, but whose honest opinions often cause greater problems than they solve.

You already know the answers to the troubles you face, you just don't know you know them. All you have to do is tune in to your own judgment, the quiet voice of your intuition echoing up from deep within your unconscious mind. This is your internal guidance system. If you let it, it will lead you unfailingly toward the light. Whenever you get a strong hunch to do something or go somewhere and you don't know why or what for, you just have a nagging feeling in the back of your mind that you should, then that's your intuition calling, with clear instructions to help point you in the right direction. Act on its promptings fearlessly, without hesitation, and you will never be led astray.

Don't waste time worrying about what the cynics and doubters are saying. Their greatest pleasure is to fire up your imagination with so many fears and uncertainties that you abandon your plans long before you ever get started. And ignore all the do-gooders, those people who shower you in their homespun wisdom, whether you want to hear it or not. Your intuition *knows* what's right for you; other folk only think they do. The moment you start viewing life through the prism of their opinions is the moment you hand over control of your career, your happiness, your identity and your destiny to the say-so of someone else.

I love criticism, just so long
as it is unqualified praise.
—Noel Coward

z

Straight zigzag: Good judgment. Only criticizes when he has something constructive to say, so his opinion is probably worth listening to. Never short of an opinion. Keen to exchange views. Even if judgments are not expressed, you know he is thinking them. Better, therefore, to invite his input than miss out on a valuable opinion.

Open figure-3 shape: Criticism is backed by wisdom. The larger the bottom loop, the greater his reserves of understanding. The writer has a singular grasp on the way things work. Combines life experience with a natural depth of vision. Turn to this person for help, encouragement and direction in times of stress.

Closed figure-3 shape: Has strong views on life, but they may be too rigid and any real wisdom is lost in the flow of opinion. This writer can tune into his intuition if he wants to and dispense good advice, but he's reluctant to trust the voice within. Prefers logic and reason, even if they do let him down occasionally.

Left-slant zigzag: Eager to point out flaws, although more likely to be motivated by a desire to get things right than by malicious intent. Critical attitude could spark conflict. Quick to find fault, slow to bless. Should try holding back and wait until someone asks for his opinion.

Right-slant zigzag: Slow to offer observations and opinions. Evaluates the situation first. If he has something critical to say, it will be carefully worded. Even then, he would rather bite his tongue than speak his mind, especially when there is a risk of offending people.

Bowing: This person has definite views on what he likes and what he dislikes, but tends to keep them to himself. He won't offer his opinions too easily, and he certainly doesn't want to hear yours. This often results in a stalemate. Leave him to get on with his life; don't force issues.

Drawn back: Shrewd and observant, with a real eye for detail. He has an opinion on almost everything. Can be judgmental, even cruel, when making assessments, though he believes it to be for the common good. Master of the withering look or the knowing wink. Intolerant.

Raised: Expectant, enthusiastic. Keen to make critical points but without hurting anyone's feelings. Just wants to be involved, like an eager dog. Believes that everything will turn out okay in the end. Underneath, he's afraid of criticism himself, so tries not to criticize others.

Curl-around 3: There is wisdom here, but it is kept private. The writer won't throw his opinions around freely, although his advice and observations will be useful when he finally gives them. A useful person to know but don't expect him to be your guardian angel.

Narrow curl-around 3: What little wisdom there is, is guarded fairly jealously. Answers are only dug out with effort. He won't wish to interfere in other folks' lives; equally, he won't want them to poke their nose into his. He is happy to know what he knows and keep it to himself.

Alphabet A-Z

A

A relates directly to a writer's sense of purpose in life. How confident is he in the decisions he makes and the actions he takes? Is he aware of his strengths and weaknesses? Does he know where he's heading, and, if so, how sure-footed is he in the pursuit of his dreams?

self-reliance

It takes great courage to plow your own furrow in life. Self-reliance means being so sure of who you are and the course you're on that you make your own rules as you go, untroubled by second thoughts and refusing to give in to outside pressures. You may look to others for guidance, but only to yourself for answers.

The reason I say it takes courage is because these days so many people seem to be caught up in a sheep mentality. Their quest is to belong to the herd, to fit in and do what everyone else does. "I'm comfortable, I'm secure—what else could I possibly want?" they say. And at first glance a no-risk, keep-your-head-down policy looks pretty attractive. What they don't understand perhaps is that each time they let someone else do the thinking for them, they give up a part of their own unique identity and with it the chance to make something really special of their life. By conforming, they're choosing apathy over action, watching helplessly as prosperity slips through their fingers and countless golden opportunities for happiness pass them by.

In the words of the Buddha, you must "Work out your own salvation. Do not depend on others." The will of the masses is very strong; whichever way you turn, whatever your goal may be, a vast battalion of mediocrities lies in wait, ready to ambush you and convert you to their go-nowhere, do-nothing belief system. Resist their advances at all costs. If you must join forces with other people, then be sure to associate only with those who can open your eyes to a better way of doing things and who talk of getting results and making a difference, rather than continually searching for the easy way out. In truth, there *is* no easy way out. There never was. The road to self-empowerment is fraught with difficulties that must be overcome through direct action based on our own judgment and our own assessment of the situation, not by looking to some outside agency to step in and solve our problems for us. So do everything you can to be self-reliant. Turn your back on the herd and always, *always* go your own way.

Footprints in the sands of time are not made by sitting down.
—Proverb

Check out the strength of the A. Does it stand tall and bold, or has it collapsed in on itself? The sturdier it is, the more self-reliant the writer is likely to be. A crumpled A indicates herd thinking. In his moments of weakness the writer falls in with the crowd instead of standing his ground.

Upright, pointed: Strong enough to weather most storms. Makes personal choices without reference to what other people might say. Listens to reason but won't give in to bullying or pressure. Controlled, circumspect, aware of his own power, capable of making independent decisions and setting his own agenda.

Upright, rounded: Easygoing and approachable. Likes to believe he has a firm game plan but could be persuaded to drift. Not so rigid that other possibilities are out of the question. Tries hard to keep a grip on circumstances, yet in some ways is content to sway in the breeze. Needs to cultivate greater resolve.

Klan hood: Under some kind of pressure. There's a lot going on, many problems are closing in. Sometimes feels like giving up and starting again. Traces of sadness and fatigue underscore an uncertain attitude. Feels bullied or imposed upon by outside world. Looking for reassurance and a helping hand.

Enlarged small a: Fairly self-reliant. Past experience provides necessary ammunition for most situations. No longer led astray so easily. Sees the world for what it is and can usually distinguish between something worthwhile and a waste of time. Reserves of wisdom indicate understanding but also a resistance to change.

Looped crossbar: Still harboring emotional issues from long ago, which get in the way of freedom and perfect action. While appearing strong and resilient, there are undercurrents of self-doubt or worry that undermine his efforts. Time to off-load some baggage.

Flyaway crossbar: Looking to others for help, support and answers. Tries to get situations sewn up alone but it just won't work. He needs to know that folks around him approve, or at least don't object. He is self-sufficient in the smaller issues but may need support for greater ones.

Backward flyaway: Burdened down. Relying too much on outdated advice and other people's opinions. Their approach sets a precedent, one that he follows and refers to constantly. He is not taking enough control or responsibility and may be passing the buck too often.

Triangle: Fiercely self-reliant, even stubbornly so. An independent thinker who ignores rational advice and goes the way of his heart. Honest, scrupulous and prone to being disparaging about opinions that don't coincide with his own. Vibrant, persistent, a real original.

Triangle flyaway: This person has a point to make. He has a natural vitality and resilience and also an agenda that he sticks to fairly rigidly. In negotiations, he gives as much as he gets and expects to receive favorable terms. He dislikes incompetence or foolish behavior.

Deflated: Moods dictated by others. The writer has handed over control to the whim of other people and is now at the mercy of outside forces. In some ways he feels beaten, and has given up on the idea of breaking free. Seeking courage and confidence to rise above the crowd.

Downsweep: Likes to think through problems independently, without interference; will not welcome others' suggestions. Brushes off external advice in case it destabilizes the situation and throws him off course. Don't offer your opinion unless he asks for it.

Albert Einstein. *A man of many brilliant ideas, with a serious analytical mind. The A is sturdy, showing self-reliance, and belongs to the kind of guy who was fairly secure in his thoughts and values. He knew what he meant even if many people around him didn't! Not a person who was blown off course too easily.*

B

Strength of character

Occasionally, you come across people who have such a strong character they just can't help making an explosive impact wherever they go. In fact, their personality seems so dominant at first that it can come across as overwhelming, even frightening. Yet stand in their shoes, see the world from their point of view, and you realize it's all an act: the loud voice, the mood swings, the demanding tone—it's a cleverly structured piece of theater designed to win attention or, more likely, to serve as a defense mechanism to keep attackers at bay.

Deep down, the pushy, demanding person is short on self-love. What looks like strength to the outside world is really a fake. True strength, the kind of inner calm or sureness that makes for personal contentment and solid, trusting relationships, comes when you accept yourself for the person you are—for better, for worse, good points and bad—and then endeavor to *be* that person wholeheartedly. People want to see the real you, not some elaborate hoax. They like to understand where you're coming from so that they can relate to you emotionally; they don't care if you're not perfect. They're not perfect, so how can they expect you to be? Besides, if you were, there'd be nothing left to strive for, would there? Life would be boring.

Be kind to yourself. Acknowledge that, although you have a whole series of flaws, you have many excellent qualities also, and these must be given their chance to shine. Remember: The rest of the world takes you at your own estimation. If you love and respect who you are, then others will, too.

Act like a lamb and the wolves will eat you.
—Anon.

B

Check out the size of the lower hoop on the B. The larger it is, the stronger the writer appears on the outside. If the hoop also happens to rub up against the next letter in the word, this means he is pushy, possibly domineering and likes to have his own way.

Average-sized lower hoop: This writer knows what he wants and expects to get it, but he doesn't feel the urge to push too hard. Won't hold back when something needs to be said or action has to be taken. Probably has natural authority without forcing the issue. He means business, and people recognize this.

Big lower hoop: Make way, he's coming through! A force to be reckoned with. Strong, pushy, often defiant if demands are not met. Drives points home with passion, making his mark and stirring others into action. Won't sit back and get trampled in the rush. Expects to be taken seriously.

Small lower hoop: Not assertive enough. Won't want to stand out in a crowd or appear overbearing. Rather insecure and unsure of personal power. Holds back. Thinks, Once bitten, twice shy. Remembers the last time, how hurt he was, and doesn't dare come out of his hole again. Needs to be more assertive.

Blunt: "I know what I know, so don't go thinking you'll change my mind"—that's the message here. Like a copper saucepan: tough, resistant, and with a surface strength that is difficult to break. Can take the heat and won't weaken. May not be too confident underneath, but hides it well.

Looped at base: Asks directly for what he wants. Not the sort to be afraid of rejection. He figures it's always worth a try. Whatever the situation, if results are needed and clear action must be taken, this is the person to get the job done.

Pulled apart: Despite his best intentions, difficult circumstances and outside pressures are causing this person to lose track of his plans. He pulls, he pushes, he hangs on to whatever he can, but it's a difficult job. He's losing it. Time to rest, reevaluate his position, and try a fresh approach.

Backsweep: The writer's view on current situations is affected by past experience and his upbringing. This may not be a bad thing, however. Conditioning and experience together can often add up to a formidable energy. Possibly wise and unexpectedly knowledgeable.

Forward stem: A fighter who pushes on against the odds. He is a driven person. Many personal issues dating back to his youth stand in the way of progress and cause him to strive harder than he should. If he relaxed and stopped pushing, he might go farther.

Rippled hoops: Feels tense and fearful at times; finds it hard not to show it. Life seems packed with awkward twists, and keeping them at bay takes a lot of energy. There are moments when he feels it's all getting to be too much. He doesn't need any more setbacks right now.

Overhanging top hoop: Not so confident; in fact, rather weak inside. Tends to play the victim and overreact under pressure. He bruises too easily and finds it hard to bounce back after a disappointment or apparent failure. This can't go on. It's time to toughen up.

Looped stem: Plenty of thought and deep self-questioning lie behind this person's actions, probably caused by incidents or conditioning during childhood. At the back of everything he does is a flood of concern about whether his actions are the right ones. Slightly confused.

Pointy: Sharp and quite persistent in the pursuit of his aims. He can be unbending and prone to rubbing people the wrong way. They may give him the things he wants just to please him. There's something uncompromising about his approach: Things do get done, but at what cost?

C Some people have a real thirst for knowledge—news, opinions, facts, trivia, anything at all. They pick up information from all over the place. Others are more choosy. They don't want to know everything, just what's relevant. The *C* is there to tell you who is who.

knowledge

You've heard the saying "Knowledge is power"? Well, that's true to a certain extent, but it's not the whole truth. Knowledge only really becomes power when it's put to good use; up to that point it's just data. If we don't take what we know and apply it positively so that it contributes in some way to the personal growth of ourselves and others, then we may as well not know it at all. You can be the greatest academic in the world or the keenest trivia buff, but if all that stuff you've got inside your head just stays there, what good can it do?

Acquiring knowledge should be an effortless joy. You learn fastest when you're fascinated. It makes perfect sense, therefore, if you plan to work at the same job day in, day out, giving so many thousands of hours of your valuable life to it, to find one that grabs your imagination and makes learning the ropes a real pleasure. In the end, whether you're happy or unhappy in your work depends on the attitude you bring to it, yet it's amazing how many people have not yet grasped such a simple truth. They just don't get it. They don't understand that work is meant to be a pleasurable experience. In their eyes, hobbies and sports are the things you enjoy; work is something else—hard labor, a necessary evil that pays the bills so you can relax and have more leisure time. But isn't this just our old friend "herd thinking" again? It doesn't have to be that way. After all, how can you be expected to give yourself to a job heart and soul if it bores you half to death?

When you're enthralled by what you do, you don't resent a single minute spent finding out about it. In fact, if they weren't paying you, you'd probably do it for nothing. As I said earlier, all of us have at least one major passion, something that fires us up with enthusiasm and takes the grind out of learning it. This passion is the key to your destiny. Leave someone else to tackle the boring stuff; you stick with what you love, and accept that by doing it you are aligning yourself with your true purpose, moving ever closer to the life you were supposed to lead.

It is better to die on your feet than to live on your knees.
—Dolores Ibarruri

C

Check out the space inside the C. The more room you find in there, the more knowledge this person acquires and the better he is at absorbing information. A C with very little space inside belongs to someone with narrow interests, who knows what he likes and sticks with it.

Average size: Bright, with an interest in many subjects. Absorbs knowledge and definitely finds satisfaction in learning, but may be a jack of all trades. Aware, unprejudiced, ready for anything. Is likely to be an expert in his field. Even if he's in the wrong job, he'll try hard to make the grade anyway.

Large, deep: An inquiring mind with a huge thirst for knowledge. A versatile, lively approach means he's able to come to grips with new ideas when others can't and adapt them to suit his needs. Could get sidetracked, if only because anything and everything is so fascinating. Needs to be a little more focused.

Shallow: Very choosy. Only interested in specific kinds of information. Anything irrelevant hits the garbage. Can spot nonsense at twenty paces. At times, this person has a limited view of the world and a narrow perspective. Could miss fascinating facts by being focused on one thing only. Should seek to expand horizons.

Looped: A loop indicates a range of preconceptions that interfere with learning, beliefs so firmly set in place that new information won't overturn them. Usually the result of experience. Life has taught this writer many lessons. Nowadays, he clings to old fears, worries, concerns and prejudices. A hard habit to break.

Small: Ignorance is bliss. Learning is not a priority. He's content to stick to the tried-and-tested and let other people tire themselves out in the pursuit of knowledge. More information only means more complication; to his mind, the less you know, the simpler life becomes.

Loop pulling back: Restricted by old ideas that still tend to color whatever he learns. He probably won't accept that he has a closed mind. Even so, he is clinging to a mass of preconceptions that get in the way of expansive thinking.

Sharp blockage: Says, "Look, I just don't wanna know, okay?" Cynical, blocked, immovable. The writer has a large capacity for learning, but the barriers are up and nothing can get through. He ought to try letting go of rigid thought patterns and to embrace a few new ideas.

Leaning over: Unhappy with developments. The more he discovers, the less he likes the situation. Just keeps on uncovering new horrors. He's trying to keep further crises at bay while tackling present problems. I guess he feels that life is out of control right now. Get a grip!

With small loop: Experience has taught this person a few harsh lessons; as a result, a small number of ideas are fixed firmly in place, never to be removed. As far as he's concerned, facts are facts, so don't waste your time arguing.

With back support: He is ready and willing to expand his knowledge but finds it difficult to modify an already hardened mind-set. He approaches new information from a very selective angle. This goes back to his upbringing and cultural influences.

Here was a man who thought he knew it all. **Clark Gable**_'s C is closed and hooked, blocking out whole wads of important information. He was fairly knowledgeable about certain subjects and eager to try new things and explore many avenues, but once his mind was made up about something, that was it and there was no changing it._

D The *D* shows how tenacious the writer can be when the chips are down. Is he the sort who keeps on keeping on until he's beaten the odds and his dreams have been realized, or does he give up at the first sign of an obstacle?

persistence

One of my mother's favorite sayings was "God loves a tryer," and in my own life I've always found that to be true. Persistence and hard work together weave their own special magic. In the words of Vidal Sassoon, "The only place where success comes before work is a dictionary." To achieve any goal, it's not enough to have a plan—everyone is planning to do *something* someday—you must also have the reserves of stamina and persistence necessary to see that plan through to a successful fruition. Nothing can defeat the person who keeps pushing on through, like the Energizer bunny, even in the face of overwhelming odds, and refuses to give up.

Of course, no matter whether your plans are magnificently ambitious or fairly safe and unadventurous, they still must be rooted in solid foundations. Why waste time and energy pursuing some half-baked fantasy that stands no chance of ever becoming a reality? Be sensible. Research your goal, test it and, where necessary, seek expert advice; then and only then move on to the next step. Because, if the foundations are weak, it won't matter how much you persist in your efforts, just one shake, one mild tremor of confidence, will send the entire structure tumbling to the floor, taking all your dreams down with it.

One other important key to persistence: Stay true to your vision. Don't be a butterfly, flitting from one goal to the next, and don't quit halfway merely because nothing seems to be working out. The results you're looking for may be waiting for you around the very next corner—tomorrow, the next day, next week—you'll never find out unless you're patient and keep going. That's what's so wonderful about life. It may be wildly unpredictable, it may be confusing sometimes and mysterious and frustrating, too, but it's always, *always* unfolding in your favor. Believe that, rely on it and, come what may, press on. God really does love a tryer!

> The heights by great men reached and kept,
> Were not attained by sudden flight,
> But they, while their companions slept,
> Were toiling upward in the night.
> —Henry Wadsworth Longfellow

D

Check out the size of the D's belly. The larger it is, the more persistent the writer will be. A big-bellied D signals a strong character, someone who won't take no for an answer. A small, narrow D usually belongs to the cautious person whose spirit of determination is low and whose resolve wavers in the wind.

Average belly: Knows when to press forward with plans and when to be patient and bide his time. Feels uncomfortable forcing other people to obey orders, but will do everything necessary to keep the show on the road. Not one to give up easily. (If the D touches the following letter, the writer is a bit more pushy than if it doesn't.)

Oversized belly: Really lets you know who's boss. Likes to stand up and be counted. Expects people to do as they're told. Overbearing, often overwhelming, this person won't stop until the job is done and the prize has been won. Pushy and persistent. In fact, he finds it difficult *not* to throw his weight around.

Thin belly: Timid, won't come out of his shell. At the first sign of a setback, his instinct is to recoil and give up. Lacks follow-through. Thinks, Achievement involves risk, risk carries danger of failure, failure would mean embarrassment, and embarrassment only endorses my lack of self-worth. So why try? An overhaul of basic life principles is called for.

Swing-around: Goes for the direct approach when dealing with people. It's the only way to get things done. Thinks, Why waste time dropping hints or beating about the bush? Believes in laying it on the line and to hell with the consequences. A certain amount of strategy and cunning may lie behind his actions.

Oversized belly, tiny stem: A lot of the writer's personality is for show. What seems like confidence on the outside is just a mask for the insecurity felt inside. Compensates for inner weakness by pushing others around and generally being larger than life.

Swept back: Actions greatly influenced by incidents and experiences during childhood or the distant past. He feels his behavior is justified because he was taught to respond that way as a kid. His persistent attitude may exist simply to prove his worth to others.

Pointy: Sharp, no-nonsense attitude. If this is not a ruthless person, then he can certainly be difficult at times, putting pressure on others to behave in a set way and do what he wants. Persistent when he has a goal in his sights. Deals with life on his own terms.

Downward, pointy: Will *definitely* upset a few people as he moves boldly, persistently toward his goals. He wants everything now and expects others to move out of the way simply because he's coming through. Impatient. Hates delays. Has an inflated view of his own importance.

Looped: Thoughts go in one direction, actions in another. There are many sides to this person, although it may not be too evident from a first meeting. Doubts and other concerns stand between him and the Big Prize. Like old tapes, they play over and over at the back of his mind.

Bull-horn: Fierce, combative, determined. Not easily defeated or thrown off course. A real fighter who goes all out to win. There is a will to survive here, which can lead to confrontations and a general stampeding over those who are not as alert or quick-witted. Watch out.

Sweep-around: A driving-force personality with fixed priorities. This writer knows precisely what he wants and is hell-bent on getting it, sweeping all before him on the march toward his chosen goal. Dramatic, hard to deflect, with motivations that could be difficult to discern.

Swipe: Insists on being the boss. Has feelings of superiority and takes others to task for their weaknesses. Driven by the best intentions, this person accepts no excuses and no shilly-shallying. Things must be done his way and preferably NOW!

Bobble: Emotional preoccupations and doubts haunt all decisions. There are reservations and uncertainties in his head, which cause him to act at less than peak performance. He hesitates a little too much and worries unnecessarily, when what is really called for is direct action today.

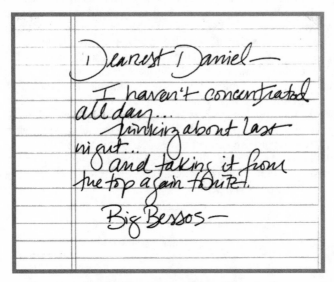

A strong, dominant individual. The enormous, bulging D's say it all—a sure sign that this woman knows what she wants out of life and no one is going to stop her getting it. Forceful, spirited and not the type you'd want to tangle with!

E

A person's whole approach to life is summed up in the way he draws his *E*. It highlights the writer's mental, emotional and sexual energies, so you can quickly tell if he has strong beliefs, inspired ideas and a healthy sex drive, and also whether he is a good communicator or a shrinking violet.

Self-expression

Many people, and I mean *many* people, for one reason or another, do all they can to suppress their deeper creative urges. It's crazy. Why put a lid on all that wonderful potential? If you want to try your hand at painting portraits, for instance, why shouldn't you? Okay, so you may not be the next Monet or Cézanne, but who cares? That's not the point. Fill your life with experiences, not excuses, and express yourself in any way, in *every* way, you can.

Hold nothing back. Be spontaneous, be bold, be outrageous, be the one who does what others dare not do! If you want to dance, then dance. If you feel the urge to write poetry but you're a lousy poet, do it anyway. Better bad poetry than no poetry at all. Let your heart have its say. Whatever your urge may be, and however ridiculous or extraordinary it might seem to other people, if it turns you on, don't sit on it, *do it*. Thousands of new and stimulating adventures are lying in wait for you right now. If you can't find the energy to do them, ask yourself, Why not? What is holding me back? Is it fear? Embarrassment? Or maybe you've fallen into the trap of thinking you're too old. If so, the only thing you can be sure of is this: While you sit at home inventing a million reasons why you shouldn't, others are out there doing it and loving it.

As long as your plans don't hurt anyone or infringe on their rights in any way, what have you got to lose? So come on! It's time to let the world know you're here, that you're happy and you're going to do whatever you damn well please while you still have the chance. Get out there—and express yourself!

Only he who does nothing makes a mistake.
—French proverb

E

Check out the overall shape of the E and, if there are crossbars, the length and strength of each one. The top bar relates to mental energy; the middle bar to beliefs and strength of feelings; the lower bar to sexual energy. If they're strong, then it's very likely the writer will be strong in those areas, too.

Curly: Spontaneous self-expression. Can be glib, but thoughtful, too. Believes that anything is possible for those who try. Doesn't give too much thought to the whys and why-nots, just gets out there and has a go. Often puts thoughts and ideas ahead of deeper feelings, but so what? Eager, enthusiastic and ready for anything.

Looped and curly: Wants to be spontaneous and taste adventure, so the spirit is definitely willing. But something gets in the way: doubts, fears, hesitation. Can't overcome the feeling that it may all be too late. Sticks to more conventional aims, ignoring anything that might cause embarrassment. With effort, could break free.

Forked: Strong communicator. Has bright ideas backed by deep feelings and wants everyone to listen and understand. Won't wish to stop talking for long in case someone else gets a word in edgewise. Lively and buoyant. If this spirit is backed up with firm action toward a definite goal, then big results are possible.

Strong, sharp: Expresses beliefs, feelings and views openly. Strong sexual urges, too. Generally unafraid of appearing vulnerable; willing to take the risk of getting hurt in order to gain better understanding of life. Lives for giving and taking, the to-and-fro of human interaction. In touch with deepest emotions.

Top crossbar crosses too low: This person is either mixing in the wrong circles or wasting time pursuing jobs or pastimes that are beneath him. He is better than he thinks and capable of reaching greater intellectual peaks, so why not take a risk and go for it?

Slithering crossbars: Brings the same energy—intensity or apathy—to everything he does. There is something vaguely enigmatic about this person's approach to life. Sometimes he doesn't care, other times he does, and very deeply, too. If so, all his emotions and urges fuse into one.

Disconnected crossbars: This person is cool and detached and, for some reason, is no longer in touch with his real feelings. Responses have been dulled by life, and are now conditioned and automatic, which leads to uninspired behavior. Needs to unravel the knots that led him to be divorced from true emotions.

Bars sloping upward: Set in his ways and won't listen to reason or others' ideas. Has a firm view on what he wants and how people should think and behave. Could stifle self-expression by being too rigid and not exchanging thoughts and feelings with others.

Long top crossbar: Big on expressing ideas. Likes to reach out and put across his thoughts for change and improvement. May use opinions as a substitute for feelings, out of fear of exposing himself to pain or exploitation. (Short crossbar means the opposite.)

Long middle bar: Speaks from the heart. Looking for acceptance and love by expressing passions and strong beliefs openly. May be argumentative at times, but only because he trusts his own judgment and feels that others should hear his heart's voice. (Short bar means the opposite.)

Long lower bar pointing up: Considerable interest in sex—doing it, talking about it and exploring different variations. Thinks of sex regularly, almost too regularly, and his libido drives many of his actions. Never fully satisfied. (Short bar means the opposite.)

Looped lower bar: Signifies inhibitions and sexual energies held in reserve. It may also indicate a possible confusion in the writer's sexuality or sexual preferences. Greater openness and a willingness to face up to any taboos would help overcome nervousness about sex. It's time to talk.

Inward curls: Protective. This person is scared of exposing thoughts, feelings and sexual needs to scrutiny or criticism. He may seem distant or reserved, even when he should be relaxed. Something inside says, "Don't go all the way. Keep something back." Needs careful handling.

F

The *F* measures a writer's ability to communicate. Instantly you can see if he is a listener or a talker, whether he puts his point across with conviction because he feels his opinions deserve to be taken seriously or if he lacks confidence in almost everything he says.

good communication

Whenever we share our thoughts and feelings openly with people we are giving away a small part of ourselves. And, as with all other forms of giving, the more generous we are and the more we try to reach out to others and connect with them, not just on a mental level but on an emotional level, too, then the greater our reward is sure to be.

Truly genuine communicators are quite rare anyway, even in these advanced electronic times, so you can afford to be a pioneer in this field. Avoid playing safe, talking only to friends or colleagues—people who are guaranteed to respond to you positively. Instead, why not take a walk on the wild side occasionally? Reach out and show interest in someone you've never met before and find out what their story is. Everyone knows something you don't; everyone can relate an experience from their own life that touches on yours. Indeed, a seemingly chance remark by a total stranger, spoken at the right time, can often open a door of understanding to provide solutions to deeper questions you may have been puzzling over for ages: "Should I move to a new job or stay where I am?" "Is it the right time to buy that car I've had my eye on?" "What should I do to find a new relationship?"

I like to think that the answers we're looking for are, right this second, out there somewhere looking for us; so the least we can do is be ready to receive them. That means staying alert. Your message could leap out at you anytime: while you're reading an article in a magazine, from the slogan on a billboard as you drive by, or even from the chance remark of a stranger in an elevator. Don't bar the door to wisdom just because you think it sounds ridiculous that a complete stranger might have a piece of life guidance to pass on to you. It *is* ridiculous, sure, but it happens time and again. Try it. Dare to step beyond the confines of the known and the trusted; lower your resistance a little and communicate! You might be most surprised by what you hear.

I'm here to live aloud.
—Émile Zola

F

Basic forward bars: Clear expression of thoughts and beliefs. Expects to have opinions taken seriously. Direct and sincere. Not the type to back off from saying what needs to be said or from speaking with genuine concern. May not be very tactful, but tends to listen before making judgments. Solid, dependable, strong.

Extended top crossbar: Extremely eager to make his point. Insists that others sit up and take notice. The expression of ideas and opinions matters more than feelings. Possibly loud, probably interfering; won't miss out on the chance to speak. Always asking questions. Personality could be overpowering at times.

Basic backward bars: Plenty going on under the surface—related to feelings, but also to regrets from the past. Has many ideas, many opinions, but he'll wait for the right moment to express them. Shows one face to one group, another to another. May be too modest, or afraid of quick involvement. A dark horse.

Curled back: Still dealing with people and issues that have been around for some time. Has much experience and brings it to bear on current problems. Communicates closely with those who have been accepted into his circle already, but may be slow to make new friends or seek the wisdom of strangers.

Bars slope upward: Just won't listen! He may agree to disagree but he'll not change his mind readily. The problem is, he genuinely believes he's right every time and is scared of being found to be wrong. The more he tries to persuade you, the less you believe him.

Downward slope: Feels weak and deflated inside. Lacks the will to resist other people's point of view and tends to go along with them rather than put up a fight. He may be too easily led and in danger of stopping thinking for himself altogether.

Looped backsweep: Spirited and go-ahead, but secretly worried that his own opinions may not be acceptable or "the right ones." Because of this, he uses other people's views to back up his own. Despite appearances, he is slightly confused, hesitant, a little troubled inside.

Tall, fragile: Feeling misunderstood. This person may waste time arguing over principles and persuading others to see reason, only to end up with crossed wires. "Why do other folk never get my point?" he bleats. Perhaps it's because he is trying too hard.

Overhanging top bar: Exposes people and their work to merciless scrutiny. His judgment can be fierce and unrelenting when he is in the mood, and his wit is pretty special, too. Analytical and usually right in his assessment, he has a matchless gift that others may envy.

Small, weak: Not really a communicator by nature. Opinions and feelings are low-key and held back when they probably should be expressed. There is much room for personal development here, but it needs to be driven by a desire to make better emotional connection with others.

Top bar curling up: Quite proud of his own thoughts and ideas; believes them to be beyond reproach. In his view, certain things he says are so obvious they can be taken as read. He won't want others to spoil the fun by criticizing his opinions, so he keeps them out of harm's way.

Top bar curling down: This writer feels exhausted through trying. All his efforts at getting his point across seem to have come to nothing, and he's slowly losing heart. Even if his ego has taken a beating he must keep going. Speak and people will listen.

Top bar overhang: Opinions shaped by the past and old conditioning. He knows many things, and many teachings infiltrate his thoughts and opinions. There is probably a desire to pass on this knowledge to others, which could be a cause of frustration if they resist.

G

The letter *G* can be used to reveal a person's attitude toward risk. Does he like taking chances? Is he eager to try all kinds of different experiences—food, vacations, music, sports—or are there limits to his horizons? Some people refuse to stray too far outside their comfort zone. The *G* helps us pick them out of the crowd.

risk

Nothing of lasting value is ever achieved without a measure of risk. No Broadway shows would be produced, no household products manufactured, no cars designed and made, no airlines would get off the ground, no businesses start up and prosper, if somebody, somewhere, didn't trust his or her hunches and take a chance.

Success is no good if it comes too easily. If everything you ever attempted to do was a guaranteed winner, if everything you desired landed right in your lap and you never lifted a finger to earn it, wouldn't you simply take it for granted? Of course you would. We all would. Eventually you'd just get plain lazy and start treating your newfound riches with contempt. Someone once said, "Without danger the game grows cold." Well, it's risk that provides that danger. Security, comfort, predictability—in a mad, chaotic world these things have their appeal, but in the end they lead nowhere, except maybe to stagnation. At all times you've got to keep moving, keep reinventing yourself and keep on taking those risks.

It needn't be anything too ambitious to begin with. You may want to try broadening your horizons a tiny bit, pushing against the boundaries you've set for yourself to see if they'll give a little. You might turn your hobby into a business, for example, or decide to learn more about stocks and bonds and begin investing for the first time, or it might be something as simple as taking next year's summer vacation in an unlikely place: giving up on Orlando and visiting Alaska instead. All that matters is that you begin loosening your grip on a few of the old habits and reclaiming your freedom to act spontaneously in new directions. Risk is all around us anyway—we take a gigantic risk just crossing the street these days—so why not grab it before it grabs you?

Risk! Risk anything!
Care no more for the opinion of others . . .
Do the hardest thing on earth for you. Act for yourself.
—Katherine Mansfield

G

✎ **Check out** the size of the G's mouth. The larger and deeper it is, the greater the writer's appetite for new experience and the more risks he will take. If the mouth is blocked up, he is less likely to try new things and could miss many positive, fulfilling experiences.

Open mouth: High risk. Open to anything. Likes to experiment, break away from the usual rut and explore new areas. If other people go along for the ride, great; if not, well, that's their loss. On the downside, he may not always make the wisest choices, but hey, you never know unless you try, right?

Closed mouth: Low risk. Not willing to break free of his comfort zone. Past experience has shown this person that risk leads to problems. The shutters are down—anything for a peaceful life. New ideas are given close scrutiny before being accepted. Needs to be more adventurous. Open that mind!

Looped: Average risk. Life has taught many lessons already. Thoughts, worries and preconceptions get in the way of a good time. Approaches new experience with a fixed mind. Not blocked exactly, more cobwebbed in old habits. Whatever the activity, don't expect him to indulge too quickly or too freely.

Bird-table: Low risk. When the top curl of the G dangles over the horizontal crossbar, then the person chooses activities carefully. The mind is open and new horizons may beckon, but there are many routes to take. Insists on careful planning before venturing beyond the comfort zone.

Narrow: Adopts a low-risk policy. Has a limited interest in new ventures and is no doubt a little short on natural curiosity. Whatever he tackles, he tends to be single-minded about it and sticks within narrow limits. He needs to get out more, frankly.

Big loop: If this person does take risks, it's only after a lot of thought and planning. Won't allow himself to move too swiftly or go with the flow in case he loses his position. Fixed perceptions mean his mind is blocked to many opportunities. Could miss out.

G on a stand: Highly inflexible on some issues. Social and cultural blocks limit the writer's horizons. He has grown up believing certain ideas are true and won't change them now, even if they seem outdated. These beliefs get in the way of positive growth.

Pulled-back mouth: Eager for change and fresh thrills, but enjoyment of new activities is often spoiled by other factors: ingrained attitudes, parental conditioning, etc. Feels pulled in two directions, forced to grab all he can while he can.

Loops top and bottom: May take risks occasionally, though many blockages stand in the path of fulfillment. Approaches life with a restricted viewpoint. Finds it hard to be spontaneous and free thinking in new situations. Old habits die hard.

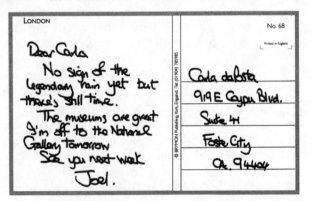

This brief postcard reveals that Joel is a very choosy, fastidious individual who's slow to take any risks, whether it's at work, at home or anywhere else. The G is large and round, offering plenty of room for absorbing new experiences, but it is almost closed, showing that everything and everyone is scrutinized carefully before he will commit himself or lend his support. A slow burner.

H

Compatibility

Compatibility can be long term or short term. Two people enter a relationship knowing they have certain basic things in common. Maybe they share the same interests, have a similar outlook on life, are both in the same kind of job—these factors and many more make up the glue of compatibility that helps bond them together. If things go according to plan, this bond will not only last, but could blossom over time into something greater and more profound.

However, as people grow older, they find their life taking off in many wild and totally unexpected directions. Maybe they switch careers midstream, make new friends, hit upon a fascinating hobby their partner doesn't like, get bored with sex, become passionate about wine—it could be anything. But it means that many of the factors that made up the glue of compatibility and that seemed so crucial way back in the formation stage of their relationship may start to lose a bit of their sparkle. Things just feel different, as though the wind has switched direction suddenly. If a marriage continues to be based on love, respect and mutual understanding, that's great, it will endure; but if it isn't, why endure the marriage?

Of course, marriages hit unexpected turbulent patches all the time; it doesn't always signal the end of the relationship. In fact, a major upheaval can sometimes give the couple a perfect chance to reevaluate their feelings about each other, talk through any problems and push themselves up to a higher level of support and understanding. But if it doesn't . . . when everything we know and feel tells us this just isn't working out anymore, when the downside outweighs the upside, when it just makes sense to pack our bags and leave, what other option is there? We must accept that one phase of our life is drawing to a close, and a fresh one, offering new relationships and wider opportunities for growth, is right around the corner waiting to begin. Then leave.

Women are as old as they feel;
men are old when they lose their feelings.
—Mae West

H

✎ **Check out** the two upright stems of the *H*. Think of them as two people standing side by side, then ask: Are they up close or far apart? Is one stem larger than the other? If the relationship is happy and well balanced and both sides feel they are still learning and growing, the two stems will be close, of equal size and joined together.

Straight, upright: Simple, balanced, loving, mutually supportive, each side sharing responsibilities equally. Two hearts beat to the same rhythm, generating strength and understanding. The glue is holding, but without either side feeling suffocated. Good and strong with plenty of physical attraction.

Right stem looped: Promises interesting times. The writer's partner may inject difficulties into the relationship. Either they play hard to get sometimes or they're of two minds: caught between committing to the relationship and wanting personal freedom. There is an imbalance here, an uncertainty that goes unspoken.

Right stem larger: Writer idolizes partner, places his or her love on a pedestal, may allow no space for freedom. There is something all-consuming about this. Unreasoning devotion. Writer takes too much on trust. Could be hurt if things go wrong. Needs to be more realistic about partner's faults and not take too much for granted.

Crossbar crosses right stem, not left: The writer uses the relationship for his own ends. Has lost heart. No longer feeling those special feelings. The love may have waned but the bond is kept alive by force of personality. Somehow, somewhere, this relationship may have lost its way. Serious issues must be faced.

Crossbar pierces right stem: Looks like the writer's partner is well and truly hooked! Strong feelings underlie this relationship. The partner may feel pinned down or trapped at times by the force of the writer's personality or attention. If so, such feelings need to be discussed openly.

High crossbar: This relationship is cemented by an intellectual connection: Shared views and an inquisitive streak create the vital spark. Fun comes from the brain rather than the heart. The writer feels uneasy letting his heart rule his head. Prefers the expression of ideas to the expression of emotions.

Diagonal: An unbalanced match perhaps, although the results may be positive. Each partner gains different rewards from the relationship and brings to it his or her own qualities and strengths. Opposites attract, as the saying goes.

Hoops on both stems: The relationship works like a mutual support system. Each partner helps the other handle problems and deal with his or her own issues. There will be moments when these people irritate each other intensely due to their respective weaknesses, but this may even add an essential spark to the relationship.

Left stem curl: This person is carrying around various bits of emotional baggage from previous relationships. The writer's partner is forced to accept these issues, since they won't go away. Old wounds may be causing pain, but the writer is not facing up to the problem. Time to move on.

Low crossbar: Strong, firm bond. No doubt sex is a prime factor in keeping love alive. If they're not having it, they're thinking about having it—a lot! Despite the partners' differences, and even though they may have widely differing interests, under the surface they have a deep connection.

Looped crossbar: The writer has problems giving love freely, openly and unconditionally. There are undercurrents and doubts, confusions and compromises. This person may even expect to get hurt, only to find that expectation fulfilled. Needs to be more trusting and less sensitive.

Stems close together: Two people who are very involved. Their interests may be narrow and their lives may be unadventurous at times, but their support for each other knows no bounds. The writer and his partner are close, and even though they may face problems they still stay together throughout.

I

An *I* standing alone tells us how much the writer needs to have other people around. Is he independent and able to make important decisions on his own or does he seek support from others and crave constant reassurance before he can take positive action?

independence

Nobody understands your affairs like you do. Nobody takes care of your hard-earned money with the same concern and enthusiasm that you do, and nobody—not even your most loving, caring nearest and dearest—has your interests at heart in quite the same way you do. What you have is all you've got, so it makes sense to look after it. Being independent means taking full responsibility for your own destiny. Once you allow people to have a hold over you and to start dictating terms—what you'll do, what you won't do, yes sir, no sir, three bags full, sir—you're lost; you become a victim of circumstance, forever needing a green light before you can make your next move.

When you are faced with a big decision, ask questions, take in as much relevant information as you can, and even consider what other people feel about it, if you think that'll help, but in the end you must make the decision alone, according to your own judgment and principles. Always be guided by your heart and surrender not an inch to convention or consensus-thinking. If you enjoy being single, for instance, and the thought of a lifetime relationship sounds like forty years in jail to you, then hang on to that belief. Under no circumstances throw yourself into married life anyway, just because all your friends are doing it and you don't want to be the odd one out. If it feels wrong at the start, then the moment you say "I do" you'll wish you hadn't. Similarly, if you feel pressured by friends to commit a wrong deed, something that pricks at your conscience and makes you feel uneasy, be independent enough and strong enough to say no. Stay true to the dictates of your intuition and walk away.

It won't be easy—doing the right thing never is—but all the approval in the world counts for zero if you earn it by betraying your principles. The truth is, when it comes to your life and what you do with it, *nobody* knows which path to take better than you do.

Not in the clamour of the crowded street,
Not in the shouts and plaudits of the throng,
But in ourselves, are triumph and defeat.
—Henry Wadsworth Longfellow

I

Check out the height of the single *I* and also how close it stands to the words on either side of it. If it is strong, tall, and is well spaced, the writer is independent and makes his own decisions with confidence. But when the *I* seems weak, or is crowded in by the words around it, you're looking at someone who needs constant reassurance.

Single line, well spaced: This person is extremely independent. Suggests clarity of thought and firmness of decision. Willing to try anything, whatever brings the greatest benefits. Plots a clear route and feels strongly enough about his decisions to defend them. Won't want to lean on others or ask for help unless it's really necessary.

Topped and tailed: Knows what makes a comfortable life and tries to stick with what's familiar. A creature of habit who prefers to mold circumstances to suit his own tastes. The longer and more striking the top and bottom lines on the *I* become, the more of a control freak the person is. Guards territory selfishly.

Looped: May crave total independence but there are other factors that get in the way. Responsibility to others may pull down this person's spirit. He has a sense of duty but also expectations to live up to. All these add extra weight and take the edge off the freedom this person would really prefer.

Dragging a weight: This writer is wrestling with events in the present while also dealing with old memories from the past. It may be the fairly recent past, but this emotional baggage ties him down. Has a desire to break free but can't. Too much has happened. It's time to clear away the debris of yesteryear and move on.

Dragging a weight, no top loop: A strong, single-minded individual. Many significant events in the past still carry an electric charge. They may be positive or negative memories, but either way the writer can't escape their effect, which creeps into his life in small but important ways.

Backward-facing: Reserves of wisdom and knowledge, with possible awareness of family and cultural history. Where this person has been is just as important as where he's going. An independent, almost defiant, nature knocked into shape by considerable experience.

Disjointed top and tail: Fixed, and yet free also. The writer sets firm boundaries but is able to remain flexible within them. He'll give new things a try and is not so tied down to routine that he can't experiment once in a while. A weird combo of being self-controlled and easygoing.

Figure-9 shape: Has a head filled with thoughts, pride, judgments, doubts, all rolled into one, and he can't shake them off. He may not want to, especially if they give him the strength he needs to get through each day. If not, he needs to throw off his mental chains.

Figure-2 shape: It takes great effort to live "in the now." This person has problems escaping the past to focus solely on the present. Experiences, both good and bad, from days gone by have made a huge impact, so it's not easy to turn his back on them. And why should he anyway?

Zigzag: The inner self is being blocked. Outside factors—work, family, money—are consuming this person's life. So much effort goes into controlling the different elements that many vital personal needs are being overlooked. Needs to slow down and let go.

Looped and curly: Tries to remain buoyant, but it's hard when there's such a lot of "stuff" to cope with, most of it caused by other people. He's striving to achieve his goals while at the same time handling a whole load of complications and problems. Manages to rise above it—just!

Fishhook: A late starter, someone who is gradually getting his act together as he grows older, though very slowly. In many ways, he is happy as he is and doesn't invite much change into his world. He is emerging from the cocoon of familiarity and sameness to make his mark.

Needle: A commanding personality, someone with a deep desire to make an impact on people around him and get his message across. His independence is rooted in childhood influences. Single-minded, with a flair for turning situations around and driving things forward.

Biplane wings: This one's a real control freak. Everything in life is carefully planned and coordinated and put in its proper place. The writer likes to be master of his own fate, so friends and family must fit in with his schemes and ideas, otherwise there could be serious disagreements.

Floppy top: Pressure is growing, threatening plans and dreams. Tries hard to maintain the status quo but it looks like things are getting out of hand. Part of him wants to let go and allow situations to work themselves out naturally, while the other part is itching to get a grip and bring them under control.

Looped, fat: Self-doubt weighs down his spirit. His mind is blurred by worries and fears, most of them irrelevant and cumbersome. This person struggles on valiantly against the odds. Although he has great potential, by not living up to it he knows he is letting himself down.

Jen my love,
ever since I spied
you at the MTV
innaugural ball
jitterbugging across
the floor I haven't
been able to silence
the passion that
overcame me. I know
that I'm an older man
but I'm hoping you
can find a place for me
in that big-heart
of yours. Until then
every time I look at
tabitha soren I'll pretend
she's you. ♡
the unrequited kurt

Valentine's message. Quite a tense and moody person. None of the letters are joined together, which usually means the writer is holding a lot of emotion knotted up inside. Also, all the I's are topped and tailed, showing that this person is rather fixed in his ways. He has definite likes and dislikes; above all, he dislikes change because it disrupts the pattern of his life.

J

If a person is pleasant, approachable and enjoys making friends, then this will be reflected in the way he draws his J. It also warns us of his attitude toward personal relationships. Does he have a free-and-easy attitude toward his partner or is he a jealous lover?

friendship

Friendship is not something any of us can afford to take for granted. It must be worked at tirelessly with the same amount of loving dedication we'd invest in any flourishing enterprise. True friends are hard to come by; they're so rare, in fact, that if we manage to find half a dozen in a whole lifetime we can consider ourselves blessed.

A true friend is someone you know you can say anything to, someone who will do you a favor without questioning why and listen sympathetically to all your troubles without standing in judgment. Friends of this caliber give you a sense of belonging; they make you feel like your life really matters to someone else. You can laugh and cry together shamelessly, take pride in each other's achievements and share your joys and heartaches both the same. They'll praise you wholeheartedly when you do well and diplomatically when you don't, and are tireless in their efforts to remain loyal and supportive through the leanest and meanest of times. True friends love you not for your money or your position or for what you might do for them, but just because you're you. Period.

Of course, many of the people we call "friends" are not friends at all; they're acquaintances. They come on a short lease, staying a week, a year, five years—however long it takes to help us in some way, by teaching us an important lesson, or even steering us away from our present course and onto a different one—then they're gone. And however painful it might be to see them go, we must not hang on. They are gypsies, after all, just passing through; we don't own them. So be wise enough to let them go. Treasure the friends who stand by you forever, and be grateful for the ones who don't. Both have their purpose.

You can make more friends in two months
by becoming interested in other people
than you can in two years by trying
to get other people interested in you.
—Dale Carnegie

J

Check out the openness of the J. Is it slung wide, like a great yawning mouth, or is it looped and closed? An open J means the writer enjoys having a whole stream of friends and acquaintances pass through his life. He's not possessive or "clingy." A closed J means the opposite. He has a few close friends and sticks by them for a lifetime.

Upright, wide open: A balanced, freewheeling approach to friendships. People come and go through this person's life without obligation or restraint. He is not possessive or jealous. Everyone is invited to the party, and they can leave when they like. Always changing friends, always surrounded by interesting people. Fun.

Looped and closed: Chooses friends carefully. The larger the bottom loop, the more people will be welcomed into the group. Believes friendships are long term and must be worked at. Seeks understanding, sympathy, frank exchanges, realistic advice and honest, unconditional love. That's all.

Top loop: Not an easy catch. Probably a good networker. Has many friends and acquaintances, but likes to know that through all the ups and downs of close relationships at least some of them will be there when it matters, as firm support and a shoulder to cry on. Feels he can handle any burden if his gang is at his side.

Looped: Hangs on to close friends come what may. Has an A-list and a B-list, all carefully chosen and kept in separate camps. Quality control is important: New friends must meet a certain standard and be of a particular type. Puts a high price on family and close relationships; nurtures them with great love.

Pointing inward: Many people pass through this person's life but don't give him the time or attention he feels he deserves. He's looking for respect and friendship but doesn't always find them. He feels unworthy somehow and people pick up on this, so his needs get overlooked.

Closed, fierce: Extremely selective about the kind of person he lets into his circle. Take care, because he may have a hidden agenda and use the people he meets to help him reach his chosen ends. Could be a good friend, but could be possessive, too. Difficult to escape his clutches.

Slanted crossbar: Feels threatened by too much attention. Suspects that people may be after something when they befriend him, so he chooses his buddies with great care. They must serve a purpose and enhance his life in some way. Keeps everyone else at arm's length.

Bottom loop, with crossbar: Keen to have friends, and lots of them, but very few get close enough to be considered part of this person's inner circle. He forms a deep bond with a choice handful of good buddies, but other links tend to be more superficial. May appear to lack warmth.

Looped, with fierce inward curl: May have been given a rough ride by friends and lovers in the past. Nowadays, he feels neglected or victimized. It's possible he's not a good "chooser" of friends, trying to get close to those who should remain acquaintances, and staying remote from folks who, in fact, would make excellent pals.

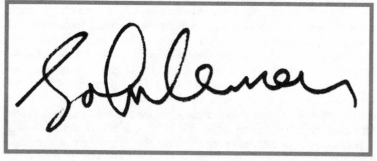

Looped, with tail: In the past, many people let the writer down or disappointed him. He has learned to be more discerning and better prepared for their vague behavior. Those he trusts are treasured now; others can go on their way. A certain regret or sadness remains, however.

Low loop: Has a very small number of special friends. They're close, they know the truth, and they can be relied upon never to "kiss and tell." Everyone else is considered transient. They pass through and have a good time, but never quite make it onto the A-list.

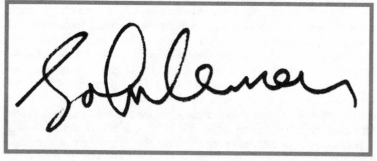

John Lennon, *it seems from his signature, was quite a humble man at heart, but also an extremely perceptive and idealistic one. The J shows that he was of two minds about the level of attention he received. His sharply observant wit was a by-product of his insecurity as well as a defense against outsiders who might get too close to the private person behind the public image.*

K *K is the letter that measures get-up-and-go. It lets you know if the writer has natural authority and is a mover and shaker. Does he inspire confidence so that others respect his decisions, or is he weak and afraid to speak his mind in case people don't like what he's saying?*

initiative

Success on any scale does not happen all by itself. Somebody somewhere has to make it happen. One person must take the initiative right at the start and set the ball rolling. And in your own life, that person has got to be you.

Each new day should be a step forward toward the fulfillment of your most treasured plans and dreams. But even if, like so many people, those "treasured plans and dreams" are still very much a work in progress and you're not clear as yet what they're going to be, don't let that stop you from taking action: Do something, *anything*, right now that you feel might be a step in the right direction. Make a few calls, ask around your friends to see if they have any bright ideas about what your next move should be, visit a library, skim through the newspapers for opportunities . . . just keep your motor running. You may have nowhere to go, but at least make it *look* like you're heading someplace. Don't sit in a chair for hours staring at the TV, hoping that inspiration will strike. Chances are it won't. And even if it does, by that time you'll feel too sluggish and apathetic to do anything about it. Once you have momentum, you need to keep it going by filling each day with positive activity. Generally, the harder we try, the clearer our objectives become and the greater our chances of success.

It's *your* initiative, *your* drive, that will make all the difference between having what you want and not having it, between a rounded, fulfilled life lived out on your own terms and years of dull routine where you just coast along, heading nowhere and achieving nothing. Life's a game: The next move is always yours.

The shell must break before the bird can fly.
—Alfred, Lord Tennyson

K

Check out how far the arms of the K reach out. A long, strong upper arm means a dominant personality, someone who uses his initiative and makes firm, independent decisions. A long lower arm belongs to someone less forceful: the strategist, who keeps his plans secret and presses ahead quietly with his own agenda.

Arms spread wide: Strong, stable, influential. A real instigator who pushes all before him, like a snowplow. Coordinates many tasks at once; nothing gets through the net. Capable of seeing the bigger picture and motivating others toward great achievement. A shepherd rather than a sheep.

Long, strong upper arm: Forceful, with hidden strengths. This person means business and won't tolerate fooling around. Imposes his will on others, expects to be obeyed and achieve results. If strong-arm tactics are masked by charm, watch out: At the heart of his personality lies a core of steel. Could bite back.

Pincers: Alert, lively and tricky. Comes at you from many different sides to keep you on your toes. Could use force of will to pressure people into complying with his ideas. Always on the lookout for new opportunities, the main chance. Strategic, clever, motivated by self-interest to achieve chosen ends. Not to be underestimated.

Large arms start behind stem: Actions fueled by a need for appreciation. Goes to great lengths to earn the blessing of others. Will seek endorsement by trying harder, using initiative, scoring points. Didn't receive enough support as a child. Felt he deserved more and still craves it even today. Could be forceful and demanding.

Small arms: Concentrates efforts in a narrow area. This person has no wish to paint on a broad canvas; it's just not his style. He gets things done in his own way without being too forceful or overbearing. Unlikely to go ordering other folks around, in case they fight back. Steady worker.

Broken arms: Slowly weakening under pressure. Trying to cover all bases, but bit by bit he's losing his way. Makes stubborn gestures to win support. Others simply expect too much of him. He is keeping many balls in the air, knowing they may crash to the ground at any moment.

Long lower arm: Hallmark of "the persuader." The type who uses charm and other well-oiled strategies to get things done. He knows they work and that people respond favorably and do what he wants them to do, so why change his technique? A beauty without being a beast.

Pulled-back stem: When decisive action is called for, this person often holds back. A voice in his head says, "Are you sure?" Of course he's not sure. How can he be when so many lessons and experiences from the past still haunt his memory? Needs to tackle doubts and be his own person.

Long upper arm, disjointed: Uses force and strong tactics without questioning why. Actions can be tough, mechanical, unreasoned and difficult to fight off. Charm on the one hand is matched by undisguised pressure on the other. May not be a bully, but he sure gets things done.

Shaky lower arm: A timid person trying to appear forceful for the benefit of anybody watching. Not convinced he has what it takes to make an impact, but he has a go anyway. Craves appreciation and respect and he may get it, too, though currently the battle is being lost.

Long lower arm, disjointed: The writer possesses a brand of fake charm that may fool some but by no means all. Empty words are used to ensure a smooth, effective operation, though wiser individuals see right through it. Dedicated to achieving results by almost any means.

Curved lower arm: Always pushing and driving others forward, sometimes nicely, sometimes with a little more edge. He knows that effective results are best achieved by simply elbowing his way through obstacles. Charm and persuasion work only some of the time!

> King Harold was the
> King who was the most
> influential at that time.

A wonderful example of K's with arms that begin behind the stem, revealing a deep craving for love. This person has an insatiable need to be appreciated and tries desperately hard to earn affection and praise. Much confusion surrounds the giving and receiving of love, and she overcompensates for this by demanding others' respect and admiration.

L

The letter L deals with taboos, usually related to sex. Some people feel genuinely embarrassed by today's open attitude toward the subject. They don't enjoy talking about it since in their opinion sex should remain a private matter between two people. Others are far less inhibited and can't see what all the fuss is about.

inhibitions

Traditional religious teachings are often at the root of sexual inhibition, though just as often these misundertandings have been handed down from generation to generation. Seeds of guilt about sex, planted in childhood, are harvested over a lifetime. Even when they've become fully grown adults and have kids of their own, some people still feel shy and embarrassed discussing the subject.

I travel to many parts of the world each year giving talks about the positive power of handwriting analysis and showing how this power can be enhanced to bring deeper meaning to our lives. Naturally, the subject of sex and sexuality sometimes comes into it, since none of us can consider ourselves fully rounded, mature human beings if we're constantly running scared of these totally natural energies and suppressing them. But the reaction to this topic when I raise it is nothing short of fascinating. You can feel the tension flowing around the room. Clearly, there are people who feel threatened by the merest mention of sex; to their mind, it carries a curious scent of danger, hinting at something decadent, unspeakable and wrong.

Taboos of any kind are damaging to the spirit, restricting our ability to learn and grow. The best way—and maybe even the only way—to rob that taboo of its power to shock and unnerve us is the same way we tackle any fear: by taking a deep breath, turning around and facing it. Just because our parents may have grown up in unenlightened times, that doesn't mean we have to be bound by their old hand-me-down views. We buy our freedom from embarrassment and fear by squaring up to these illusions, by daring to think the unthinkable and maybe even do the undoable—whatever it takes to express ourselves openly and in a way that honors our deepest feelings.

There is nothing the body suffers
the soul may not profit by.
—George Meredith

L

> **Check out** any loops within the letter *L*—these show pockets of concern and maybe even inhibition. It could be a long-term hang-up about sex or other issues, or the loop may simply represent current reservations felt by the writer.

Right angle: Likely to have broad, even liberal views on sex. May not always talk about it, but there are no fears about expressing feelings. Prepared to be sexually open and giving and also to receive freely in return. Whether this attitude translates into physical performance is another matter entirely, but at least the spirit is willing!

Base loop: Certain subjects—sex, drugs or other issues—cause discomfort and are not being confronted. Unwilling to discuss them directly or to compromise principles. Finds it hard to throw off childhood conditioning and make up his own mind. Was taught that certain activities are morally wrong, and still believes it.

Top and base loops: Unable to release tensions due to fear. Too much self-questioning and thought get in the way of full enjoyment. "Am I good enough?" "Is this right or wrong?" "Am I really interested anymore?" Inside, he probably seeks full freedom of expression but can't let go. Time to loosen up and indulge those fantasies!

Kinked: Appears open and easygoing on most issues, but there is self-doubt here. Thinks, Can I really live up to expectations? Or he may even be questioning his sexual preferences right now. He's constantly tripped up by his own indecision about what to do. Should explore further and broaden his horizons. If it feels good, do it.

Overgrown: Indicates an inflated promise of sexual performance. This person seems inviting and attractive, but part of it is just an act. He's hungry to prove himself and to give and receive affection. Probably great fun in many ways, but there could be a price to pay.

Narrow, deep: Hard to understand and even harder to satisfy. Specific appetites must be met, but what are they? It takes effort to reach this person's inner depths, and it could be a while before his needs and desires become clear. Probably worth waiting for, though.

Wide open: Eager to sample many kinds of sexual experiences. A free spirit, naïve in some ways, with indiscriminate tastes and few rules. Anything goes. May find it difficult to make the ultimate bond with partners, if only because his demands are nonspecific. Not easy to pin down.

Loops with flipper: Taboo City! Guarded, defensive and—be warned—fairly shockable also. The writer remains closed to many valuable ideas and experiences that would open his eyes and mind. He's shy of experimenting, so don't suggest it. And don't go too far!

Shallow right angle: Uninspired. A slow-burn interest in anything physical or erotic. Whatever he thinks about such things, he keeps it to himself. Open-minded to a degree. Doesn't believe in telling the world how he gets his kicks and doesn't care how anyone else gets theirs, either.

Top loop: May not be inhibited exactly, but he has doubts about letting it all hang out and being too outrageous. Approaches drugs, sex and other taboo areas with certain reservations. When he's in the right company, he might surprise you. Generally not as open as he seems, though.

Tall stem, short crossbar: Thinks and talks a little too much, without doing anything about it. May intellectualize about sex and moral issues, but these are just words. In the end, he's probably a bit slow to experiment and put his wildest fantasies to the test.

Short stem, long crossbar: Very little thought goes into the sexual process or principles; he just gets down to it and does whatever he feels like doing. Driven by natural impulses, he won't get hung up on the moral question. He knows what he likes; others should keep their nose out.

M

The M reveals how much control the writer exerts over himself and his emotions. Does he allow relationships to take their natural course or is he the type to lay down strict rules? In other words, does he insist on having everything his own way?

Self-control

One of the biggest challenges we face in life is to be completely honest about ourselves—who we are, what our good and bad points might be, the nature of our sexuality and, above all perhaps, the strength of our feelings—but as we've already seen, this level of honesty doesn't come easy.

Women generally are more comfortable expressing their emotions than men. To the average male, feelings are vague and unpredictable things that can't be contained or defined, or understood the way, for instance, football or cars can. In fact, in a perfect world (perfect for Mr. Average, that is!) there would be a firm line drawn within relationships: It would be the woman's job to take care of all that feeling stuff—nurturing, supporting, caring and sharing—leaving the men free to play out their hunter/gatherer role: earning money, fixing the garage door, playing baseball with the kids or whatever else fits their "guy" job description as they see it. Mr. Average wants to be in control, and he'll often go to extreme lengths to stifle his true feelings rather than release them and risk making an idiot of himself. Underneath, he may be the sweetest pussycat on the block, but if word gets out that he's gentle and caring, everyone in the neighborhood's going to think he's a wimp. Or so he believes.

Now, I know this isn't true of all men. I also know there are women around who share the same fear of letting go of their feelings. Yet by trying to be so controlled all the time, we miss out on so much of the joy and drama that go with the free expression of emotion. Just as a great painter may use every color on his palate to produce a great work of art, so we must be unafraid to display our feelings spontaneously in their every subtle shade and hue. After all, why restrict ourselves? Why sketch lightly on the canvas of life when, with a little more effort, we could produce a masterpiece?

Only the mediocre are always at their best.
—Jean Giraudoux

M

Rounded, two hoops: Strong urge to build lasting relationships based on real emotional freedom and plenty of give-and-take. Mutual and supportive, with each partner fulfilling an agreed role. There is a unity here—strong, with a firm, loving bond that may falter occasionally but is unlikely to break too easily.

Jagged: Controlled, inflexible, cool, immature. The writer needs certainty and predictability and tries to lay down rules for the relationship. He must understand the territory and what's expected of him before he can relax. Insecure about showing emotion. Looking for love but is never really able to enjoy its fruits.

Looped: Writer brings a whole load of emotional baggage to the relationship. This makes contentment difficult. Unable to get a steady grip on emotional responses and enjoy the moment for its own sake; too many other factors—self-doubt, worries, problems, fears—get in the way. Time to let old wounds heal.

Hooked: Cultural influences play an important role in the writer's approach to marriage and relationships. This person comes with many views and expectations already in place. The writer's partner must accept this and adapt to it or there may be trouble ahead, as they say. Could be restricting and even confusing.

Single hoop: Can't handle gushing displays of emotion. Not interested in sharing deep passions with any partner. What counts is friendship, having a buddy, someone by his side to share his interests and life's little ups and downs.

Splayed-out hoop: Probably believes that his relationship is the best it's possible to get, but without appreciating that greater depth of emotion and understanding would generate larger amounts of happiness. Dismissive of those who suggest it's all too superficial.

High left stem: This person is living according to standards set by someone else, usually his parents. He brings these demanding principles with him into any relationship and expects his partner to fit in with his own rules. Could be difficult to live up to, and friction may result.

Tight hoops: This kind of involvement lacks spirit, breadth and imagination. As a couple, they're afraid to explore the bigger emotional picture. They stick to the familiar, the unrisky, and endeavor to avoid anything "dangerous" at all costs. There's too much pent-up emotion.

Really *tight hoops:* Signify really pent-up emotions. Many feelings are being suppressed, and many thoughts go unspoken. The sharing experience has become an endurance test, lacking the electrical charge that got it started. Excessive self-control leads to frustration.

Left hoop large, right hoop small: The writer is the guiding force behind the relationship. Whether his partner likes it or not, he regards himself as the cornerstone and therefore as more important. Could lead to dependency. Control issues need to be talked through.

Small: Regular and controlled. Yearns to break free of restrictions and experience deeper emotion, but it's hard to escape a lifetime's habit. There is room for growth here. The writer would benefit from switching his attention from work, watching TV or whatever, to how he might be more fulfilled within relationships.

Plunging right stem: This person takes great care to protect relationships and keep intruders out. He's happy with the way things are. Sees the family as a strong, independent, supportive unit and wants to keep it that way without outside interference.

Springy: A free agent—free in spirit at least, if not in reality. Likes to do his own thing, which may mean bending the rules a little and hoping not to get found out. Possesses a certain amount of roguish charm, but can be selfish at times, too. He's not as much fun as he thinks he is.

Two balanced, rounded hoops: A simple but profound connection underlies this loving relationship. The couple will be supportive, emotional and relaxed, comfortable with their mutual giving and taking. If they work on it, they have the recipe for success and happiness.

Jagged edge: Bold, self-sufficient, but possibly a tough individual to love at times. The writer likes to control relationships and be the stronger half, rather than give too much ground and risk being considered a weakling. Parents have a lot to answer for.

Wriggly: Where the two hoops stand apart, you're looking at two people who may appear to be close but in many significant ways are not. They have their own lives to lead, their own interests and friends, yet somehow they manage to keep it all together. Good if it works.

Margaret Thatcher. *This gigantic M shows the importance of the family unit. It says, "My relationship is the mainstay of my life and I'm going to protect it." She seeks companionship and loyal support from loved ones rather than gushing emotion. A practical and down-to-earth woman.*

> How does the writer handle criticism and rejection? That's what the N all about. Is he a fairly stable, confident person? Does he take it in his stride because, underneath, he has unshakable confidence in himself and his actions? Or does he withdraw into his shell every time he meets with opposition or hears the word *no*?

dealing with rejection

Nobody likes to fail, and nobody likes being rejected. Indeed, rejection is often the cause of our most painful childhood memories: your first girl- or boyfriend dumping you; that time you got dismal grades in class and your parents went crazy; the day you were dropped from the school team just before a big game. This stuff hurts. And yet the effect it has on you depends not so much on the experience itself, but more on your *perception* of it.

Opportunities are like doors, hundreds of them, stretching out into the future before you. Some—a few—are unlocked, ready and waiting for you to enter. These are your doors, they are the ones that will lead you to greater fulfillment and understanding, and they're just standing there, waiting for you to step inside. As for the others, well, they're closed and locked. Someone else holds the key to those. Trouble is, you can't say which ones are which; at first glance they're all fairly alike. The only way to know for sure is by twisting the handles until you find one that gives. For most of us, that means an awful lot of handle-twisting! But rejection is simply a natural part of that process; it's about making discoveries, nudging your way forward an inch at a time, finding out what is right for you and what isn't. What might seem like the most crippling rebuff may actually turn out to be a real smart move by the universe, a sign that the road you're on is going nowhere and that you should try again someplace else.

So always try to be philosophical about rejection. Take it in your stride. Don't flinch, and certainly don't go on condemning yourself as second rate or a failure just because someone else doesn't appreciate your gifts as much as you do. Instead, be persistent, raise your sights and keep on twisting those handles.

The only way to avoid making mistakes is to gain experience.
The only way to gain experience is to make mistakes.
—Anon.

Check out the overall structure of the *N*. Is it balanced and upright? If so, the person is probably well balanced and all the pieces of his life are fitting together nicely. If the *N* is distorted, or the right-hand stem stretches upward, then the writer lacks self-assurance.

Upright, strong: Confident enough to take the rough with the smooth. Quite stable and resilient. A mainstay for those who are not as self-assured or capable and who need someone stronger to cling to. Could be unshakable in a crisis, but he must take care that others don't sap his energy or become dependent.

High right stem: Afraid of rejection. This may be the result of early physical punishment: "Don't hit me! Don't hit me!" Or he may have been bullied as a child and still fear being cornered. Takes steps to avoid pain—may tell lies, adopt devious tactics or pass the blame on to others. Confidence is shaky. Needs to be more assertive.

Tunnel: Plenty of spark and resilience. Has an inner sense of his own worth coupled with a belief that anything is possible. Even if this person has butterflies in his stomach it's hard to tell. The urge is to keep going and take risks. Believes that good things come to anyone willing to work hard and try. So he keeps on trying.

Spread apart: Keen to take on extra responsibility, but may have too many fingers in too many pies. Weakened by lack of focus. Shoulders the burden of blame for others. Outside factors impose on his time and undermine his ability to achieve. Looking for an escape route, or at least a chance to get his breath back.

Looped: Has many beliefs and principles, drawn from life experience, which provide a backdrop to his strength, understanding and approach. They equip him for dealing with people and offer something to fall back on when things aren't going right. He finds this very reassuring.

 Squeezed: Struggling too hard to reach for his chosen goals, rather than enjoying benefits closer to home. Hates blame, and hopes to avoid difficulty by turning a blind eye to many tough situations. Could afford to broaden horizons without overstretching himself.

 Backward: This person has become a prisoner of his own methods and attitudes. He may have made decisions in the past that are now coming back to haunt him. Whether or not this is so, a defensive approach is necessary to protect his operations from exposure to the light.

 Bulbous: Appears strong, and is powerful enough to convince others that he is, but this person feels insecure inside and compensates for it by demanding that people value his efforts. Crumbles if weaknesses are exposed. Unable to take rejection. Tough when dealing with others.

 Tunnel with left curl: May be a little too confident. Wants the world to see that he's surviving okay and everything's under control, but it could be a prime example of "Pride comes before a fall." He may well have everything under control, but double-check all the same!

O

showing love and being vulnerable

There isn't a person alive who, deep inside, doesn't yearn to be wanted and loved, valued for who they are and appreciated for what they do. Every one of us is searching for connection. Yet many people, and this is particularly true in our big cities, have given up and stopped making the effort. Experience hasn't been kind to them, and they're now so afraid of being wounded or taken advantage of that they build a wall around themselves, using cynicism and tough, hard-bitten attitudes to fight off attackers. It's not much of a life. In fact, it's not really living at all.

If we lock up our heart, burying the weaker, more sensitive side of our nature just in case we get hurt, then we're denying ourselves many of life's greater privileges—love, kindness, affection, goodwill—qualities that are available in abundance and are ours for the asking, if we'll only take the risk. Vulnerability is *a good thing*. Being able to open up and show care and concern for others is *a good thing*. And lowering our defenses so that others may show care and concern for us *is a good thing* too. When those defenses are down, we not only appear more sensitive and sympathetic, we also make ourselves far more attractive to outsiders. At long last, people begin to pick up on our natural warmth. And because we seem accessible and nonthreatening and present no danger to them, they feel comfortable moving in for a closer look. In effect, we become a magnet, pulling in new friends and lovers from all directions.

None of us can remain spectators forever. Even though we've played the game many times before and been defeated, that's no reason to stand idly on the sidelines. We've got to let our vulnerable side show. Of course there are risks. And of course we may suffer losses along the way. But never as many as when we don't play at all.

Help thy brother's boat across and lo!
thine own has reached the shore.
—Hindu proverb

O

Check out the size and roundness of the *O*. Something large, like a dinner plate, suggests a highly vulnerable character, someone willing to take the risk of being hurt in the name of experience and growth. A small, tight *O* could, in certain circumstances, indicate a hardened heart.

Large, round: This person's defenses are down. He's trying to protect his weaker side but doesn't always make a good job of it. Sensitive, open and honest, with genuine feelings. There are times when those emotions just can't be stifled and they'll flood out, possibly catching others off guard.

Looped: Smart and suspicious. This writer has heard all the lines and been through all the situations, so he's not going to fall for the same old tricks. Part of this person is unreachable. He's afraid of exploitation and doesn't want his weaknesses to show. The love he gives is genuine as far as it goes, but more is possible.

Tiny, cramped: Playing safe. Unlikely to go wild with emotion or let others get close enough to do any damage. Could be missing out on a wider range of emotions due to his fear of getting hurt. Hates the thought that he might be vulnerable. Happy to sacrifice greater happiness if it means escaping heavy losses, too.

Left loop: Fighting life on two fronts: trying to move forward but is held back by the burden of old experiences. These may be his own or a by-product of parental trauma (divorce, abuse, etc.). Wants to be free to share feelings openly but something gets in the way. Isn't it time many of these blockages were removed?

Top flipper: Cool, casual. Reaching out for acceptance, yet probably quite choosy about who gets the keys to his heart. Prepared to risk all for love, but only with the right person, and finding that right person, someone good enough to make the grade, could take a little while.

Top flaps: Afraid of rejection and the pain of being let down. Can't bear to go through all that stuff again. A lot of water has passed under the bridge, and this person appears to be drowning in it. The time has come to be braver. Don't give up. Step back into the fray and start taking risks.

Open, disconnected: Too busy, too pressured to really get a handle on emotions. The writer is pulled this way and that all the time. He appears vulnerable, but it's not deliberate; it's probably due to a lack of focus and a life out of control.

Capped: Plenty of raw emotion lurks under the surface, but only a small part of it ever rises to the top; a lot of feelings are kept hidden and never expressed. His actions say one thing, his emotions another. Some people may find this person difficult to understand.

Squeezed: Other people's concerns are absorbing his time, or maybe he is taking more of an interest in their affairs than he should. In either case, he needs to clear more space for himself and work on increasing his own sense of self-worth. Real love is worth the extra effort.

Split in two by loop: Hidden depths and reservations divide this person's loyalties. Keeps part of himself hidden and only shows the side he wants everyone to see. He might wish to share himself more, but something forces him to hold back. It takes time to get to know him.

Such a large, sensitive handwriting. This person is very shy, emotional and defensive, but compensates for her weaknesses by putting on a grand show of personality. The size of the O indicates a heart that is tender, giving and easily wounded. She gives her love freely and offers warmth and nurturing to others in large amounts.

P

The *P* shows how fascinated the writer is by the world around him, and in particular by the affairs of other people. Does he keep his ears open for the latest gossip about friends and colleagues, or is he more self-absorbed, the sort who only takes a real interest in what's going on if it affects him directly?

Curiosity

People just love it when you show an interest in them. If you can turn your attention away from your own life and onto theirs—their work, their relationships, the way they've decorated their home, their dog's health problems, anything—I swear, you'll soon become the most popular person in the neighborhood. By turning the spotlight onto others, you make them feel important, and people *really* love to feel important.

It doesn't have to be an obvious thing you do—just look and sound interested. Ask questions and show that you're absorbing the answers by asking further questions off the back of what they've told you. Avoid playing the silly cat-and-mouse game where you constantly drag the conversation back to your own life. We all love talking about ourselves—nobody's affairs are of greater interest to us than our own—but people who talk only about themselves usually end up talking *to* themselves. We all know our own news anyway; what we don't know is what the other person has to tell us. So let them speak. The reaction you receive will always be positive. In fact, more than positive in most cases—they'll adore you for it.

Curiosity is a great way to keep yourself up to date with what's going on. What it *isn't* is a cheap excuse to go nosing around in other people's affairs. Positive interest is one thing, prying is another. Handle secrets delicately and in confidence. Don't fall into the trap of using what you've learned as evidence against the person or to bad-mouth others. What goes around comes around, remember? As a rule, always try to be first with a hearty endorsement and last with a hurtful word. You'll never regret it.

Your friend is the man who knows all about you, and still likes you.
—Elbert Hubbard

P

Standard-sized nose: Observant. Likes to know what's going on, but would never see himself as the nosy type. Bursting with a wealth of information on a range of subjects. Eagle-eyed. Won't miss much of what's going on, so don't try to fool him. Unlikely to probe too deeply into others' affairs—unless there is some very good reason, of course!

Huge nose: Curiosity—big time! Obsessed with finding out more and staying ahead of the game. Keeps asking questions. This could be distracting. Lacks focus, so nothing gets explored in any great depth. Brain works like radar, picking up signals from all directions. Needs to develop a longer attention span.

Looped stem, small nose: Has a lot on his mind. Problems prevent him from looking outward. He is wrapped up in his own affairs; other people's troubles are secondary. As a child, he may have been taught not to interfere in anyone else's business. So don't expect the latest gossip from him, because he just won't know.

Flattened nose: Not interested in people's lives or beliefs unless they impact his own in some way. Doesn't care what's going on—it's none of his business. Certain things matter very much, but they're all personal. Curiosity levels are low, so he'll never be the neighborhood gossip king.

Nose in the air: Exudes natural superiority. Has a keen eye for what other folks are up to, but manages to keep watch without letting them know it. Has a great belief that his morals or values are the right ones, and he'll protect them ruthlessly. Not to be underestimated.

Pass-back: Always has an answer for everything. The buck rarely stops here; someone else is to blame. Never acts without a good reason, although others may find that reason less than convincing. Absorbs information that might be useful and stores it up for later use.

Bloated: Has a lust for knowledge, particularly gossip. Afraid of missing anything; likes to be told what's going on. Could lose ground, however, through taking too much interest in things that don't concern him. Others may resent this person's untimely intrusions.

Pointed: Sharp and efficient and doesn't miss a trick. Nothing gets past him, so don't try. Even if you do succeed in concealing the truth, he will find it out sooner or later. Suffers no nonsense. He wants to know, and he wants to know *now*!

Pulled back: A person with plenty of curiosity, but who doesn't want others to think he's nosy. Feels guilty when he probes too much, though he can't stop himself. Something in his head says, "Don't do it." He's really straining at the leash, hoping to pick up tidbits of information.

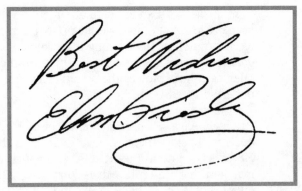

Here's a guy who never misses a trick! **Elvis Presley** was an extremely curious person—about everyone and everything, to the point of being extremely nosy and interfering. Glitz and pizzazz on the outside clearly hid emotional insecurity on the inside. He feared that others were plotting and scheming behind his back and so felt he must keep his finger on the pulse at all times. A man with many things always on his mind.

Q

Common Sense

Emerson once wrote, "Common sense is as rare as genius." I have two friends who are living proof of that statement. Both are totally impractical: They can't cook, have no idea how their VCR works, they won't even drive a car in case they lose concentration and run under a truck! Nothing ever works out for them. Whatever the situation, give them even half a chance to foul things up and they'll manage it somehow. It's like a gift.

But why? Why are some people better at handling life's complications than others? In the case of my friends, I can explain it quite easily. Both come from fairly wealthy backgrounds and both had parents who loved them so much they spoiled them with every luxury imaginable. Because they had maids and helpers who did everything for them, they consequently never got to learn the basic practicalities of life. In some ways, it's the meanest trick parents can pull on their children, to pamper them excessively when they're young. Setbacks, accidents, disappointments—these are key lessons in the human learning curve. Only by figuring out the answers for ourselves do we develop into fully rounded, capable adults later on.

Common sense is an intuitive sense, one that draws on your memory of past experiences. It works a bit like a muscle, improving and growing in strength the more you use it. So obviously the greater the pool of experience you have to draw on, the more resourceful you become, until finally, faced with any problem, large or small, you don't flinch or back down. Instead, you simply tune in to your intuition, your common sense, and say, with the confidence of one who has traveled extensively through life's more tortuous byways, "Leave it to me. I've been here before—I know what to do."

Experience—a comb life gives you after you lose your hair.
—Judith Stern

Check out where the Q sits on the line. If it is perched upright, then you know the writer is practical and down to earth. But if it floats above the line he has an impractical, dreamy streak. A Q that has sunk below the line means the writer may possibly be a bit too sensible.

Round, on line: Quite a wise person, someone who has accumulated a lot of experience down the years and is confident of his actions. The advice he gives tends to be well thought out. Willing to learn from wiser people, but their advice must be sensible and honest. He's sensitive to people's needs and responsive in a crisis.

Floating: Many of the writer's ideas lack a sense of reality. Always keen to move on and explore. Could leave tasks unfinished in his eagerness to switch to the Next Big Thing. Difficult to control or advise; probably thinks he knows best. Easily distracted by schemes that sound attractive but may not work out. Needs grounding.

Under the line: A practical person who has set himself up as a bit of an oracle, even a know-it-all, and is now finding the weight of responsibility too great. Or else current pressures are taxing his reserves of patience and diplomacy. Wants to be helpful, but people just take advantage. Needs greater independence.

Open-sided: Has a basic foundation of wisdom and understanding, but isn't sure how to use it. Too busy learning lessons and experimenting with what's possible to settle down and figure out the small print of life. Probably knows what to do in a crisis, but would never claim to have all the answers—which is a wise move in itself!

Held down by tail: This dreamy person is forced to keep a grip on reality, but it's not easy. Something is pinning down his free spirit. He wants to fly away, yet circumstances dictate otherwise. This is not a bad thing, although I guess he won't see it that way.

Split by loops: On the surface, the writer seems to have his act together, but in reality he may not be as smart as he looks. He has reservations and uncertainties about what he does, so double-check before letting him loose on your home improvements.

Oversized: Seeks to be the great comforter. Wants to be admired and trusted, but he may not know as much as he thinks he knows. For the sake of being accepted he is willing to be all things to all people. Be careful about letting him take over your life with well-meaning advice.

Tiny: Limited wisdom. Concentrates on what he knows and does what he can with what he has. If he has a practical side, this may shine through quite often, but he is not blessed with the breadth of experience to advise others on anything but his specialist subject.

Long tail: All kinds of serious issues underlie the writer's present attitude and mood. He may be a little humorless due to the pressure he feels. Goals and dreams are being punctured by factors beyond his control. Don't criticize his efforts, or he could snap.

> Once upon a time ~~there~~ was a King and Queen. They had a son and a daughter and a dog called Woof. They ruled ~~together~~ for over fifty years and lived happily ever after.

A Q that is full of despair at other folks' incompetence. See how plump it is and how it is sitting really heavily on the page? There is no lightness here, nothing carefree, just a realistic, down-to-earth person existing in an environment where everybody seems to depend on him to come up with the answers (something he secretly enjoys, no doubt!). He feels burdened and exhausted.

R

R is a high-energy letter, bursting with the will to get things done and make an impact. But it can also in certain circumstances be a symbol of someone who hesitates and can never make up his mind. It is this conflict within all of us—between the go-getter and the shrinking violet—that makes the R so fascinating.

taking action

Action is the magic ingredient in any recipe for personal fulfillment. It announces to the world that you're no longer happy to sit around passively, either waiting for "the right moment" to arrive to start building toward your goals (it never does) or for someone else to walk in and start achieving your goals for you (they never do). Ideas, dreams, plans, good intentions, all count for nothing in the end and are destined to remain empty fantasies, pleasant but pointless, unless you get out there and do something to capitalize on them. Action makes a difference. Channeled constructively and consistently toward definite and desired ends, action stirs up a whirlwind of positive energy around you, creating exactly the right conditions for miracles to occur.

There is no such thing as luck, and nothing happens by chance. You get "lucky" the moment you quit hesitating, quit digging a hole to hide in, and say, "This time it's for real. I'm not going to stop until I reach my target." The instant you're committed, as soon as you sound like you mean business, that's when Providence sits up and takes notice and when your winning streak begins. From then on doors that may have been closed to you when you tried them before are unexpectedly thrown wide open. Strange coincidences—events you can't fully explain—start happening almost routinely: Somehow you always seem to be in the right place at the right time, perfectly positioned to take advantage of new opportunities that drop right into your lap.

Whatever your goals and dreams, if it is right for you to achieve them, then no power on earth can stop you. Nothing stands in the way of someone who knows what he wants and who is prepared to invest his every last ounce of energy in making it a reality. When persistent action gets to be a habit, the impossible doesn't just happen now and then, it becomes the norm.

An ounce of action is worth a ton of theory.
—Friedrich Engels

R

✎ **Check out** the size of the "nose" on the R. If it is fairly large, you know the writer has already got the action habit. Nothing puts him off his stride. A small nose, on the other hand, suggests a more timid approach, someone who thinks long and hard before making his next move.

Average-sized nose: Here's a person who balances spontaneous action with careful planning. Won't be rushed into unwise decisions; must have all the facts first. Once prepared, though, he moves purposefully. Can be decisive if he has to be and knows a good opportunity when he sees one. Great stuff.

Oversized nose: Two possibilities: either a brilliant improviser who gobbles up any problem you can throw at him and spits out an impressive result, or a bit of a loose cannon who acts impulsively. Either way, the writer breezes through trouble, making quick decisions according to changing conditions.

Long leg: Like a blind man's stick, this is used to test the ground, preparing for all kinds of possible outcomes. Cautious, steady, hesitant and slow to commit unless sure of his facts. Can be a slow mover and hold everyone up. Equally, it may be his saving grace. Useful to have around, even if he is cautious sometimes.

Looped: Before moving forward, he takes many considerations into account: What kind of impact will his decision have? Is it the right thing to do? Too much deliberation could get in the way of positive action. May be suspicious and eager that others shouldn't get the upper hand. Needs patient handling.

Small nose, short leg: Hesitant, lacks confidence in his actions and fears negative outcomes, so he tends to do less when he should be doing more. Too humble and sometimes ineffectual, due to poor self-esteem and a lack of assertiveness.

Curl-around: Actions are unpredictable at times. What seems like a simple operation will be made more difficult by the writer's different take on life. Clear decisions are muddied or thrown off balance by his unconventional attitude. The reason is rooted in his upbringing.

Undersweep: Strategic and clever; someone who plays the game of life well and who gets the lowdown on rivals or colleagues before making a move. He probably knows what you're going to do long before you've done it. Always seeking to gain the upper hand.

Stunted: This person lives his life on other people's terms. Their views and decisions take precedence over his own—unjustly. He should break out of this cycle of weakness and regain control of his circumstances. Personal power doesn't come automatically; it must be claimed.

Springy: Buoyant and playful, and not really taking life's obligations seriously. The writer lacks commitment to his plans; most things are done on a trial-and-error basis. Claims to enjoy the gamble of not knowing outcomes, but may be losing out as a direct result.

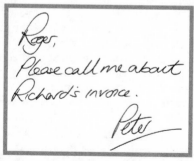

Wow, what a go-getter! Those large, bulbous R's are a sure sign that this man rarely plans his moves; he prefers to skip the formalities and dive right in, thinking as he goes, enjoying the thrill of never knowing what might happen next. Sparky, bursting with initiative, someone who enjoys a date with danger every now and again.

S

An *S* measures the impact a person makes when he enters a room, the way he holds himself, the personal energy and authority he exudes, the vibes that other people pick up off him. Presence is part confidence, part charisma, and, rather like style, you either have it or you don't.

presence

Most of us have what it takes to impact the folk around us positively. If you feel good about yourself and give off an aura of being happy with the kind of person you've become, then this unshakable spirit will be transmitted to everyone you meet. Most times you don't have to say a word; they just know from the way you walk, the tone of your voice, even the look on your face, that there's something special about you, a certain strength of character that sets you apart from the rest of the crowd.

But before this can happen, before you can be fully respected and appreciated by others, you first have to learn to respect and appreciate yourself. Believe in your abilities and so will they. Love who you are and that love will be mirrored back to you many times over. After all, if *you* can't feel good about all the great things in your life, how can anyone else be expected to?

That doesn't mean you must be in love with yourself, so euphoric about your looks or your talents that you can barely drag yourself away from the mirror each morning. The real key to self-love is being grateful for everything you are and everything you have right now and letting that gratitude shine out of you like a beacon for all to see. Confidence in oneself inspires confidence in others. Of course it can inspire hostility, too. The world is full of insecure people who regret not going out and doing something more constructive with their lives, and who will resent you because you did. Ignore it. Don't let their problem become your problem. You have a Divine right to be happy, that's the bottom line, but also a Divine duty to stand up and make your presence felt. So let your life mean something. Go all out to make a positive impact wherever you are.

It's the hinge that squeaks that gets the grease.
—Malcolm X

S

Alert, strong: Although this person may not turn heads or attract excessive attention, he's firm and steady in his approach and will earn respect through persistent action and his high level of resolve. Likes to have his own way, but is probably not the type to sacrifice his principles to get what he wants.

The harp: If the harp is large, this person is a driving force, someone who is captain of the ship. He has an attitude that commands respect. It is up to the writer whether this energy is used positively or negatively, but his spirit is undeniable. A small harp has the same spirit, but is more contained.

Looped, upright: The writer is so determined to work toward his goals, come what may, that others have no choice but to sit up and take notice. On the outside he might seem unsure of his direction, but he usually gets there in the end. Not always charismatic and not the sort to make compromises, but he can be effective.

Blocked: Fiercely independent in thought and deed. Convinced he is right and everyone else is wrong. Always follows his own hunches. If others follow them too, great; if not, he doesn't care. Generally impatient and stubborn. Creates an aura of personal strength that only a fool would argue with.

Pulled back: Plenty of activity, though much of it is for show. Driven by a need to get results. Could be stubborn and act without thinking at times. Sticks to his principles, always trying to do his very best. He's sensible enough to rein himself in if he goes too far.

Small, gentle: Happy to stay in the background a lot of the time. Short on charisma, but probably big on analyzing situations and working out a strategy. Unlikely to fly off the handle and behave strangely. This person does not have a deep desire to make an impact.

Head down: Difficult to reach. Wily, hesitant, doubting. External performance disguises deep thought and reluctance to accept new ideas. He's content to sit back and wait to be persuaded that your arguments are better than his. But expect an uphill struggle.

Flat top: This person has been around and seen it all before. Brings a certain attitude and spirit to situations, and this makes an impression. May appear cool and untouchable, but is really just watching things happen from a position of knowledge and experience.

Blocked, leaning forward: A real dynamo. Always moving, always taking the initiative, chasing his goals. The writer manages to create an aura of momentum and activity wherever he goes. When he is on the case, there's no stopping him. Look out, he's coming through!

Tiny loop: Has a fixed agenda and makes this plain from the start. If you go along with it, great, otherwise there could be a battle of wills. Experience has taught him many things, and nobody is going to un-teach him overnight. He knows what he knows. Just accept it.

*Forget the wimpy, weepy, clueless character he played on-screen, in real life **Stan Laurel** was quite a strong person: friendly, open, with plenty of personal presence. He knew his own mind and had fixed ideas of what he wanted out of any situation, as his huge looped S shows.*

T

It's always good to know whether or not a person is emotionally stable, especially if we're meeting him or her for the first time and have no idea what to expect. With a *T* you can often tell if the writer is a well-rounded adult or if balance and maturity still elude him.

stability

Nothing about life is ever fixed or guaranteed, however much we may want it to be. We inhabit a universe of unceasing change, and because we do, anyone who comes along exuding conviction and an aura of balance and good sense and who seems to know where they're heading will quickly build up a loyal following.

Have you ever been faced with a situation where your whole world was turned upside down virtually overnight by some freak happening, something that came at you right out of the blue? I know I have, and it sure doesn't take much—an accident, a fire, a flood, a death in the family—to upset all your best-laid plans in an instant. Because of this, and because there are times when the world around us seems to be speeding out of control with no one at the wheel, people are looking for comfort; they want to hear a message of hope. They need hope in the same way that kids, when they hear a grisly fairy tale, need reassuring that the evil witch is only make-believe and everything is going to turn out fine in the end. And whether the message we seek comes from a political party, a preacher, an astrologer or some ordinary Joe in our own community who just sounds as though he knows what he's talking about, it doesn't really matter—large numbers of people will buy into it.

Stability is therefore a quality that's highly prized. It's really just another offshoot of faith, something that's open to everybody and comes from deep down within us. Even when situations turn ugly and everything looks bleak for a while, we can overcome the phantoms of fear and self-doubt by staying calm and keeping our faith: faith in ourselves, faith in the future, faith enough to know that perfect answers to our problems always appear at the perfect time and that, like in the fairy tale, everything usually turns out fine in the end.

Put your hand on your heart and feel it beat.
It is saying, "Quick! Quick! Quick!
Only a few years at the most. . . .
I beg of you not to squander life."
—Billy Graham

T

✎ **Check out** the angle of the top crossbar. If it is level, the writer tends to be fairly responsible and well balanced. Sloping down to the left means that his childhood years still have an effect on his judgment and stability, whereas if it slopes down to the right, then the writer feels weighed down by the rigors of life.

Level crossbar: Someone with a fairly well balanced view of life. No doubt sensible and dependable. Others look to this person to be strong in times of trouble. He may not always want to help, but he gives the impression that he knows what to do next. The longer the crossbar, the stronger his grip on situations.

Left-hand slant: Childhood years had a great influence. His youth was either a golden time or just made an unusually strong impression. Either way, this person is still sorting through issues from those early days and hasn't yet emerged as a completely self-contained individual. Give him time—he's working on it.

Right-hand slant: This person is treading a fine line in his everyday life and constantly trying to maintain a steady balance. So many personal matters have not been worked out. Feels humble, even victimized at times. Guards the vulnerable side of his nature from attack while he unravels many knots from his past.

Oversized crossbar: Usually the sign of a control freak. Whether it's straight or slanting, if the bar is long and overshadows other letters, then the writer likes an element of predictability, sureness and continuity in his life. He's got a strict handbook of rules, which others are expected to obey—or else.

Wavy crossbar: Feeling pretty good on the whole and wants you to know it. This person has survived with plenty of inner strength intact. The youth and the adult have combined to make a fairly carefree individual these days. Long may it continue.

Wavy crossbar, split stem: This person is feeling the conflict between being a responsible adult and indulging the inner child. There is a tug-of-war going on in his subconscious mind: responsibility to others versus commitment to self and personal growth. Which will win?

Flopping: Pressures are growing and the world feels like it's closing in. Outside factors have arrived to shatter the writer's peace of mind. He is resisting it all he can, but it looks futile. Time to relax and get a new perspective on problems. Are they really as important as they seem?

Looped: One who aims for the stars and tries to set a good example, but to do so he must keep his deepest beliefs and principles away from damaging influences. There's a clash between confidence and self-doubt. He keeps pressing on but wonders how long he can stay in control.

Swept back: Approaches life with a strong belief system already in place, coupled with plenty of spirit. Influences from the past form a mainstay in the writer's world. He looks back with affection and wonder at the distance he has come and how well he's survived.

Top and bottom loops: Shows commendable spirit on many levels. This person believes he's got his act together. Certain issues remain unresolved, but that won't halt progress. A smart operator who deserves recognition for personal achievements—and knows it.

Floating crossbar: Imaginative, even inspired at times. Reaches out with his mind beyond the normal everyday world around him and pictures what could and should be. May have a reputation as a dreamer and is probably a little out of touch with reality, but hey, what's wrong with that?

T *holding up an* h: A supportive person, someone who was brought up to believe that helping others is a good and natural thing to be doing. Reliable in a crisis. Enjoys solving problems for people and nurturing their spirit during the bad times.

A beast of burden. Throughout this handwriting there are signs that this person supports and directs others (just look at the t in "there"). Her disconnected crossbar on the T in "TV" demonstrates an imaginative mind, which, because the crossbar is curved, is being dragged down by outside forces. This person wants to be a free spirit but is pinned down by obligations and duty to others.

appetite for life's joys

Life, as they say, is what happens to you while you're making other plans. Often we get so caught up in the small stuff of everyday living that we lose sight of what really matters and why we're all here in the first place.

One thing's for sure: Life is not about paying bills. It's not about stress or bank loans or credit card repayments or passing exams or nursing our aches and pains, or worrying whether the neighbor who borrowed our lawn mower will ever return it. These things have their place, but they don't matter. Not really. Not in the great cosmic scheme of things. They're small-fry, minor distractions, like so many of the other pressing matters we routinely devote hours of our lives to each day—a part of living, for sure, but by no means the main part. The philosopher Horace once wrote, "Count as profit every day that Fate allows you." That means finding the joy in each and every living moment and letting none of it go to waste.

Life is an event, one that should be packed with wanton indulgence. You're here to have fun. You're here to laugh and dance, sing and joke, and go wild occasionally too when the mood takes you. Life is about saying yes more often than you say no, smiling a whole lot more than you frown, being kind to others when it's least expected, giving generously of whatever you have without calculating the price or hanging around long enough to accept thanks. It's about being bold with your affections, loving as many people as you can openly and unconditionally, whether they love you back or not. In other words, it's about being *alive*. Time is short, your days are numbered, so get moving and cram in as much as you can. As Horace also said, "Seize the day; put no trust in the morrow." Exactly. Start living, start *now*.

In your quest for gold,
strain not your eyes scanning fertile fields afar.
For gold is right at hand.
—Henry Knight Miller

U

Check out the throat of the *U*. The deeper and wider the space inside the letter, the greater the writer's appetite for life. Ask: If this were a cup, how much liquid would it take to fill it? A lot or only a little bit? The *U* should be deep enough and wide enough to hold all the experience and excitement that life has to offer.

Average depth: A sign that this person is still searching, still trying. Open to all kinds of new experience and always ready for opportunities to expand horizons. May have a number of fixed perceptions about life, but he's still in the market for a good time. Wants to experiment, and is ready and waiting for the Next Big Thing.

Broad: Afraid of missing out. This person wants it all. Sometimes spreads himself a bit thin and may not always investigate ideas in any great depth, but he manages to cover a lot of ground. Frustrated by secrets. Wants openness and accessibility every time. Believes that life is for living and there's no better time to live it than now.

Tall, narrow: Restricted vision. Has settled snugly within his comfort zone. "Better the devil you know . . ." could be his motto. Seeks predictability and avoids adventure wherever possible. Intense, and missing a lot of fun. Focuses on molehills until they become mountains. Needs to take a fresh look at life.

Curl on left stem: Smart and switched on. Thinks he knows a thing or two about the world. Has lived long enough to try many different things. Not easily led astray. Nowadays he's slowed down a bit and is saving his energy for the really good stuff. Likes to have fun, but prefers it to come in bite-sized chunks.

Looped: No longer taking as many risks with life. Worries and second thoughts get in the way of a good time. There will be a reason. Maybe some events turned sour in the past, or maybe other people have come along and spoiled the fun. Either way, this *U* is a slight danger sign. Time to go back to basics. Think Life, not Strife.

Closed: Guarded. Closed off. Possibly ready for big new horizons but is scared of the sky falling in along the way. What this person has been through in recent years has taught him to climb back inside his shell and avoid further excitement. Wrong move. Get out and explore.

Leaning to right or left: This person has his own peculiar slant on life. Takes what he wants and leaves the rest. Fine; a discerning viewpoint, but often the things we hate doing are the ones that educate us most. Why limit ourselves, especially if it means missing out on a good time?

V V is best imagined as a container waiting to be filled—with experience, opportunities and stepping-stones to a brighter future. But first the writer must leave the past behind and be prepared to strike out in a new direction. How good is he at letting go when the time comes to move on to pastures new? The V knows.

out with the old, in with the new

Anyone embarking on a process of renewal must also be willing to let go of the past. You can't have one without the other. That means taking a good hard look at all the "stuff" you've accumulated over the years— old possessions, old values, old habits, even old relationships—and deciding which, if any, still have a special meaning to you and which have outlived their usefulness and deserve to be thrown out.

Often we only realize how imprisoned we have become by all the stuff in our life when it's too late. It can take years of feverish hoarding and possessing, buying and storing up before, finally, we see the light. Suddenly it hits us: This doesn't feel right anymore. There are so-called friends around us who simply don't belong there; possessions we never got around to using, yet they're still taking up floor space; feuds and disagreements with family members that have gone on for far too long and need to be resolved before another week goes by. In every case, whether we're talking people or things or even issues, the rule is this: If you no longer get excited about it, get rid of it. Keep pouring milk into a bowl and eventually it will fill to the top and spill over, right? Well, the same goes for you. You can only open yourself up to receive more of the good things from life if you first empty out a little of what you already have to make room for it.

Be brutal as you cut back on the waste. If you've got clothes in your closet that you haven't worn for six months or more, give them away. If your garage is overflowing with junk you haven't used in years, dump it. Dump it all. Draw a line in your diary and write: *No more junk!* Start clearing away the debris. Do it joyfully, knowing that by ridding yourself of yesterday's clutter, you are making way for bigger and brighter tomorrows.

How is it possible to find meaning in a finite world, given my waist and shirt size?
—Woody Allen

Check out the spread of the *V*. The wider it is, the more willing the writer is to accept new elements into his life: new friends, new opinions, new experiences, etc. Tight-*V* people are usually hesitant about letting go of the old. They like what they've got and intend to keep it.

Generous and wide: This person is always on the lookout for bigger and brighter experiences. Welcoming and warm, vibrant and open; nothing is barred, no possibility excluded without careful thought. Open-minded but also perhaps flighty. Hard to pin down. Always expecting something even better to come along.

Clenched: Feels suspicious when other people recommend things. Only indulges in the latest craze after much thought. It's hard to win this person over with badly thought out arguments. He's got a narrow frame of reference and tends to hang on to the old because, well, "you never know when you might need it."

Curved inward: Not ready for spring-cleaning yet. Guarded, illusive, self-serving in some ways. Hangs on to what he's got for fear of losing it. Won't be drawn into committing to a new policy or way of life without asking many awkward questions. Thinks, If something sounds too good to be true, then it probably is. Old ways are best.

Hooked on left: This person thinks he's got life all worked out. Knows what matters and what doesn't. Feels that change is unnecessary because he was shrewd enough to discard all the unnecessary stuff a long time ago. However, may not be as smart as he thinks. Long-term attitudes and beliefs could do with a revamp.

Small, angular: Where did the adventure go? This person tends to have restricted space in his life for anything new, however wonderful or enticing it might prove to be. Keeps to his own narrow agenda and sticks with what he knows. Needs to expand his range one step at a time.

Looped: Resisting change. Has reservations about the future and probably also about anything new or untried. Because he's unsure of where he's going, he sticks to trusted methods and erects obstacles to progress. By asking too many questions he is only adding to the confusion.

Chubby: There's a lot going on in his life, so no wonder the writer feels like protecting himself. He's bombarded by influences from all sides. Although he wants to experience new things, he also wants to hang on to what he's got. So many choices, so little time to make them!

Tail on right: Enjoys the good things and wants to share them with others. Always ready for change, to try something a little bit different. Eager to be the first to indulge in a new experience so that he can tell friends about it afterwards. (The wider the V, the truer this is.)

Tail on left: Probably needs his wings clipped so that he doesn't behave too impulsively. Marches into unexplored territory with an open mind and enjoys being persuaded to try something new. Wants to experiment and to learn. (The wider the V, the truer this is.)

Narrow, two tails: Not yet ready for major upheaval. Seems slightly bored with life or resigned to never getting exactly what he wants. Things don't seem to turn out the way he would like. Wants more good times, yet is unwilling to let them in somehow. His own worst enemy.

W's are about the way we compensate for our insecurity. If you need to know whether someone is naturally vibrant and full of life or if it's all an act and the person is just trying to get himself noticed and earn praise, then *W* often has the answers.

Showing off

One of the few things you can be sure of in life is that every person you meet feels insecure about something. Insecurity is that peculiar short straw we pull when we're born, what we call our "weak spot," which gnaws away at our confidence and has to be fought and conquered every day of our life. Some get hung up over their looks, some are shy, others have a whole host of neuroses and fears that click in automatically the moment they walk into a roomful of people. Everybody has *some* kind of insecurity, and everybody compensates for it as best they can.

Take the show-off, for example, the compulsive attention grabber. Show-offs will dance on tables, tell jokes, boast to friends about how much money they're making or how good they are with the opposite sex—anything to convince you they're just a little bit better than they feel inside. Behind the performance, though, this kind of person is deeply insecure. He really doesn't like himself very much, and because he doesn't, he figures you won't like him either. It's a common problem, one that begins at a very early age. For whatever reason, his parents never gave him the level of affection he craved and needed so badly. He felt unappreciated, starved for love, and because of this, he's sentenced to a life spent clawing back that love in other ways.

Of course, confident people enjoy attention too—everybody likes a pat on the back occasionally—the difference is that they don't *need* it. When you're confident, intuitively you know you're doing okay anyway. If others praise you for your achievements, great, but it's not essential, and you certainly won't run around panhandling for compliments.

Showing off is not a bad thing, but it's not a necessary thing, either. Generally, it's easier to be impressed by someone when they're not struggling so hard to impress you.

People that seem so glorious are all show; underneath they're like anybody else.
—Euripides

W

Check out the spread of the wings on the *W* and also how tall they are. The grander and larger the *W*, the more of a show-off the writer is likely to be. An oversized *W* usually belongs to a person who needs praise, someone who simply must get attention before he can feel good about himself.

Large, rounded: Makes quite an entrance. Sweeps in, oozing enthusiasm, shooting off instructions. Wants to appear strong and take control. Trouble is, this person may not feel strong where it matters: inside. Hides weakness and insecurities by putting on a show. Wants to be liked but may try a bit too hard.

Tall, angular: This person means business. Any insecurity is well hidden behind firm, constructive action. May dismiss people as fools, believing them to be incompetent, and decide to take charge himself. Impatient, always striving for a better way, showing other folks how it should be done. A natural leader.

Tall and compact, with flippers: Fairly secure. Makes good use of other people to protect his weaker side from becoming too exposed. Tackles jobs alongside colleagues and friends, carrying them on a tide of joint enthusiasm. A good family person who contributes to a spirit of unity and togetherness.

Small, cramped: An undersized *W* of any shape sometimes indicates shyness and modesty, or just a small-time personality. The person may well be insecure; alternatively, he may not need to compensate for insecurities because he is content being low-key and feels he has nothing to prove. If others don't like him, that's tough.

Splayed out: Feels insecure due to a number of confusions that still spill over from his childhood years. Could be hard to handle at times as a result, and may push people too far or seem demanding. He doesn't mean to; it just comes out that way.

Bulbous: Constantly seeking endorsement and encouragement. Wants others to follow his lead and acknowledge that he's a winner. But does he feel like a winner inside? Maybe not. He will be defensive if criticized. At heart, he just likes to be liked and accepted.

Pulled back by tail: Cultural factors, acquired knowledge or even a sense of stability drawn from childhood ground this person's ambitions. He feels limited and even tied down. There is a strange combo of motivations here: part indulgence, part restraint.

Jagged edge: Hung up about many issues, which may not be obvious to outsiders. He is sharp and demanding, and probably has another agenda; in a crisis, he ropes in other people to save his own butt. Can be difficult and hard to figure out, but is worth having on your side.

Flattened out: Much is said, but with little impact. A lack of real imagination or drive, or both, causes a lack of focus. Deep down, behind the surface froth, this person doesn't know which way to go, but he's hoping to disguise the fact. Take nothing at face value.

Looped: Makes an impression, but probably not the one intended. Outer strength, if any, hides worry and confusion. Can never commit 100 percent because too many considerations have to be taken into account. Other people get in the way!

Tall middle: Bursting with knowledge and a sense of his own importance. The writer is eager to put his point across and impress anyone who will listen. Likes an audience and likes them to think he knows what he is talking about. Unfortunately, others may see through his act.

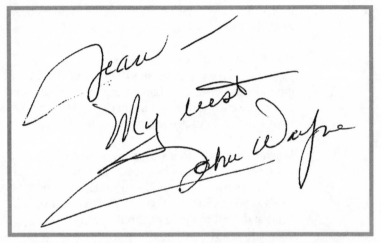

John Wayne's W: *Obviously a man who wanted others to respect him for what he stood for: all his views and principles. The handwriting reveals someone who had buried many painful emotions from the past and kept them out of sight in order to appear strong to the outside world. That large curl on his W shows he could be difficult and defensive if criticized.*

X

The letter *X* only really applies when the writer is already in some kind of ongoing relationship. The precise way the *X* is drawn, where and how the two diagonal lines cross each other, offers a fascinating insight into the level of closeness this person feels with his partner.

togetherness

Togetherness means different things to different people. For some couples it might mean being around each other twenty-four hours every day, sharing each second, never missing a beat of their partner's life. Others may swing the other way: They have a looser understanding of what it means to be in a close relationship, treating it more like an easygoing friendship with each partner doing his or her own thing, even dating other people once in a while if he or she wants to.

Open relationships do happen, and they can work fairly successfully, although I guess for the rest of us this level of openness would be profoundly unsettling, almost like not having any relationship at all. The general idea of togetherness is committed mutual involvement—the chance for two individuals to support and nurture each other, to share their interests, their joys and sorrows, fears and hopes, with someone they care deeply about. The time we spend together is the time when we find out who we really are, individually and as a couple, and how much love we are able to give; and the deeper we go with this love, the more we explore it, the more we build up a credit of trust and understanding so that, during times when we're apart, no suspicion or doubt arises. We know we can trust our partner to be faithful and true and rely on him or her not to jeopardize the relationship by fooling around.

Relationships built on a foundation of love, mutual trust and understanding are built to last. They can go anywhere and overcome anything. There is no problem too great, no issue too complex that it can't be talked through and worked out somehow. As separate individuals we may feel fearful and unsure of ourselves sometimes, but when we're together we are strong, and getting stronger by the day.

There is nothing so easy but that it becomes difficult when you do it reluctantly.
—Terence

Check out the length of each slash that makes up the *X*. The slash from top right to bottom left— / —represents the writer's own sense of how the relationship is working; the slash from top left down to bottom right— \ —represents the way his or her partner views the situation.

Firm, solid: Two people working in harmony toward common goals. The relationship boasts an inner strength, which glues it together. Mutual support and understanding lead to healthy, open communication. They have respect for each other's space, but they're in it together and ready to see it through as a team.

Long right slash: Close as a couple, but there is an imbalance within the relationship somehow. Either they are two very different people who, together, make up a solid, rounded whole, or else the writer is putting too much effort into the image of "togetherness" when really it just ain't there. Time to reevaluate their roles.

Long left slash: The partner's own emotional stability is the backbone of the relationship, setting the agenda, securing a smooth ride. Many details are dealt with by the partner so that the writer is free to attend to a different range of responsibilities. This can work provided it is by mutual consent. Otherwise ties need loosening.

Back to back: Striving to uphold values of a strong family relationship. Both sides have their own peculiarities, their own rough edges, which need to be smoothed away. Even so, there is a definite understanding here, a willingness to be loving and strong and not allow petty arguments to get in the way of a good time.

Right loop: On the surface the relationship might seem fine. Behind the scenes, though, many basic problems persist. A lack of trust or commitment slowly corrodes the core as time goes by. The writer is currently questioning the value he places on his relationships.

Low cross: Two people busy chasing a variety of outside interests. The lovey-dovey stuff is kept to a minimum to make way for more exciting things. The bond may be superficial in some ways but the varied social life keeps the spirit of togetherness alive.

High cross: What goes on in the home takes precedence over events outside. A sturdy structure based on understanding and trust, hiding many details that might never be revealed to the outside world. The relationship has built-in defenses against unwanted intrusion.

Tipping over: The writer has given up power within the relationship and feels a little helpless right now. He suspects he may be losing ground or even losing respect but is unsure what to do about it. Self-esteem issues are at the root of this problem. Needs to take steps to regain control.

Mass of loops: Usually indicates confusion and possibly unhappiness within a relationship. The writer and his partner are battling it out for territory, control and understanding. Fine if there's give-and-take, otherwise expect friction.

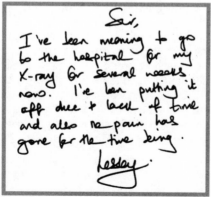

This woman is either desperate to keep a floundering relationship together and on the road or else she has no partner currently and is trying too hard to find one. The long right-to-left slash on the X in "X-ray" denotes an excess of initiative. She is putting too much effort in and getting very little comfort in return.

Y

gratitude

In our mad scramble to get more of the good things we want, it's tempting sometimes to overlook all the wonderful things we have right now. Sure, circumstances could be better—they can *always* be better—but let's not forget how great they already are.

There are no rigid rules for expressing gratitude: You can speak it, write it, think it or demonstrate it with a generous deed. The method itself is unimportant, just so long as you take a few moments each day to appreciate the many blessings in your life. However, one method of showing gratitude that always works is prayer. Praying is a powerful technique, one that opens up a gateway for earnest personal communication between you and the universe. There is nothing particularly mysterious, or even religious, about this process. All it takes is a few moments of focused silence, a break in your day when you're alone with your thoughts and can say a simple heartfelt thank-you for all the many pluses in your life.

Gratitude works. Look on it as your "Open, sesame" to a brighter future, drawing to you improved career prospects, more loving relationships, a limitless store of prosperity and abundance, all the glorious benefits and bonuses of life, which are your divine birthright but which can never become a reality if you constantly grumble and whine about how bad your life is, or how nothing ever goes right for you. Where's the point in complaining? Instead, give thanks every day, for the small things as well as the large. Keep working at it until you have turned your world around and proved, as many millions before you have proved, that the more grateful you are for the things you have now, the more things you'll have to be grateful for in the future.

The most delightful advantage
of being bald—one can hear snowflakes.
—R. G. Daniels

Y

✍ **Check out** the sweep of the arms on the Y. The wider they stretch and the higher up they reach, the more gratitude the writer will show for every new stroke of "luck" that comes his way. It doesn't matter much what the tail of the Y looks like, as long as the arms are big and wide.

Upright, outstretched: This person has a champagne spirit, enthusiastic and exuberant, and shows unqualified gratitude for each new day. He wallows in good fortune when it arrives, never missing a chance to give thanks for the wonderful surprises and twists that open up before him. A pleasure to be with and great fun.

Bent, angular: Slightly reserved about claiming the whole prize, though he's still willing to compete. Likes to live for today and to make the most of whatever opportunities come along. Might be more choosy than most. Appreciates the good things, but doesn't expect too much in case he's disappointed. Happy in his own way.

Large, with tail: Very much in control; probably not open to all this talk of prayer and gratitude. Believes in working hard to get results and making your own luck. Finds enjoyment in life but never receives as much as is available. Many doors remain closed or hidden, and this person never even realizes they're there.

Looped tail: Fun, and shrewd with it. The writer has a very firm idea of what makes him happy. He doesn't just fall for the first trick that comes his way. He is a fighter. He goes for what he wants and is grateful for what he's got. Could be excitable and enthusiastic, yet keep it under control in case others mistake it for weakness.

Small, angular: A down-to-earth, basic attitude without frills. The writer is no doubt grateful for the good things in his life but is unlikely to make a public song and dance about it or show it in a spiritual way. This is a realist who is not expressing gratitude as he should.

Petite: Modest expectations ensure modest returns. Shows gratitude, though without grand gestures. Behind the scenes the writer is not entirely sure of his spiritual entitlement; he feels that survival is a matter of luck and wits. Needs to open his mind and value the good things.

Disjointed: Takes much of life's bounty for granted. Hasn't truly appreciated all the wonderful things in his life; as a result, many opportunities for expansion and enlightenment pass him by. Should pay more attention and resolve to count his blessings in future.

Looped stem: Still sorting out his life issues; too wrapped up in daily problems to appreciate the bounty of riches that's on offer. Many private concerns and doubts are kept at arm's length. "Enjoying life to the full" is still on his to-do list, and he fails to see the bigger picture.

Wide bowl: Trying to squeeze as many events into a single lifetime as possible. Takes on hundreds of responsibilities, tastes a wide range of subjects. In danger of burnout. His shallow knowledge stretches a long way.

Craig,
Brenda called for you this lunchtime — please call her back, it's urgent. You have the number.

At heart, this is a fun-loving individual who wants to enjoy life and give it everything he's got. His Y, however, is bent and angular, telling us that despite this desire to live it up, something holds him back. Maybe experience has taught him that "all that glisters is not gold." He is happy, but not as happy as he could be if he let go of doubts and cynicism.

Z The Z can be used to identify a writer's qualities as a leader. Does he make his own firm decisions confidently, expecting others to follow, or is he the type to wait and see what everyone else does before taking the first step? In other words, is he a shepherd or a sheep?

leadership

Not everyone wants to be a leader. Many of us take one look at all the risks and responsibilities involved and know for sure that it's not a role we care to play. But even if you don't want to take charge and are happy running with the crowd, then at least take a place at the front where all the action is. Don't straggle behind somewhere, aimlessly bringing up the rear.

Whenever you can, show people that you stand for something. Speak your truth out loud with as much conviction as you possess. Others may not always welcome or endorse your opinions, in fact they may actively oppose them sometimes, but if you pack passion into what you say, you will nevertheless be respected for doing what so many others will not: standing up and being counted. If necessary, you must be prepared to peel away from the crowd and strike out in a totally different direction from everyone else, if that's what it takes to fulfill your destiny. Conformity is easy—there's no courage involved, just compliance; but being different, standing apart from the herd and doing your own thing, now that takes courage on a grand scale. After all, who wants to be an outsider? Human beings are pack animals; we need to feel a sense of belonging and the comfort of working jointly toward a common purpose. Even so, if remaining on the outside is the price you must pay for staying "master of your fate and captain of your soul," then don't quibble, pay it. It's a bargain!

Never abandon your beliefs or climb aboard someone else's bandwagon just for the sake of being popular. Compromise is easy, but living out your life knowing you have compromised when you should have remained strong and stood your ground, that can be real tough.

Never give in, never give in,
never, never, never, never—in nothing,
great or small, large or petty—never give in, except to
convictions of honor and good sense.
—Winston Churchill

Z

Check out the size and stature of the Z, and also the way it is leaning. To the left means this person is his own boss: He's happy and willing to take positive action, if necessary without consulting others. A slant to the right belongs to someone who listens to what friends and colleagues have to say and believes in rule by committee.

Upright, angular: Alert and decisive. Takes note of what others are saying, evaluates circumstances, then acts. Any impulsiveness will be counterbalanced by a natural sense of timing: when to take action and when to sit and wait. A strong pair of hands is on the tiller here. Ready for anything.

Forward leaning: Could be impulsive and make decisions on a whim, perhaps selfishly. Believes fast action brings fast results, but is he fully prepared? Plans may not be thought through. He could overlook the downside and disappoint people. Seems strong, the kind of person worth following, but may be dangerous to know.

Recoiling: Believes in consultation. Takes advice, listens to both sides before deciding what to do next. Prefers diplomacy; happy to change strategy if it will produce better results. It's the end that matters; the means are negotiable. Others may feel the urge to trust this person. Behaves like a captain, inspires confidence.

Figure-3 shape: Good at looking after his own affairs and being independent; may not be so good at leading others or making bold decisions. Actions hindered by doubts. Can be firm, can be effective, but is better at taking care of interests in a small arena than setting the agenda for an entire army of people.

Small: Territorial and wary. Will not go out on a limb without very good reason. This person fears reprisals and therefore is slow to come forward. He tries his best not to get involved unless it's strictly necessary. Clearly, he needs to be more assertive and daring before others will trust him.

Duck-billed: Impatient for action. Can be tough on those who break the rules or disobey him. Wants explanations, and they'd better be good! Brings a certain style and approach to problems, which others will either love or loathe. Often misunderstood, perhaps, but seldom ignored.

Fierce slashing: Has an impressive style. Bit of a show-off really, someone who likes to strut his stuff and let others see how it should be done. Plenty of pizzazz, but this razzle-dazzle may detract from what is really going on. In the end, he may not achieve as much as you think he has.

Figure 2: Straining to see the bigger picture, reluctant to dive in too quickly and become involved. Remains aloof from the battle, hoping not to get his shoes dirty unless it's absolutely necessary. Could seem weak or cowardly when, in fact, he is really just appraising the situation first.

Crossed and looped: Makes a better deputy than a leader. Likes plenty of information before making decisions—maybe even too much. All factors are taken into account and he keeps plenty of information in reserve. Difficult to get a grip on what he's up to some of the time. Clever.

Troubleshooting Guide

The emphasis throughout this book has been on the practical side of analyzing handwriting. For the sake of making it easier to use, I've deliberately skipped as many rules and principles and as much tedious theory as I could get away with. Who enjoys reading theory, anyway? However, for the sake of completeness, and for the benefit of anyone who makes it this far and is still having problems, here's a brief selection of the most popular questions I get asked at my seminars, together with the answers I usually give out.

"My writing changes all the time. In fact, I'd say I have about five different styles when I write. Does that mean I'm strange?"

Of course not. We all write in many different ways. Our handwriting can vary according to the mood we're in, how stressed out we feel and so on. Even the conditions we're writing in can make quite an impact: There will be a huge difference in style, for instance, between a scribbled grocery list you attach to the refrigerator and the careful way you write a birthday card. So don't worry—it's perfectly okay to chop and change.

"I've been looking at a piece of handwriting just now and some of the letters on the page aren't in the book. Why not?"

Imagine just for a moment how many millions of people there are in the world—in this country even—every one of them a unique individual with his or her own unique history and circumstances. If each person has five different ways of writing, like you do, then it is not going to be possible to cater to all those variations in a book of this size. Humans are way too complex ever to be categorized or pigeonholed completely, and we should be grateful for that. It's this complexity that makes us so interesting and gives our lives infinite richness and diversity. However, having said that, a large number of possible variations are included here, enough to give you at least the flavor of a person's character.

"I've studied graphology a little myself in the past, and I don't remember the stuff I learned back then being very much like the material in this book. Why is that?"

Because this material was researched over very many years, quite independently of traditional graphological teachings. It has proved its accuracy a thousand times over, and indeed can often achieve results that the old analytical techniques cannot. Which does not mean that everything you learned before is redundant. Old-style graphology, in the hands of a gifted expert, can be a wonderful tool. But this system is less technical, less complicated and—to be perfectly honest—much more fun. Three excellent reasons for using it, in my opinion.

"Can I totally rely on the definitions of each letter in this book and take them as gospel?"

That's a difficult one. I'd like to say yes, and most times I've found these definitions to be extremely accurate. But again I come back to the issue of uniqueness. We're all so different. Our handwriting is as peculiar to us as our fingerprint or voice pattern. Nobody ever writes the same way we do. We don't even write the same way we do from one day to the next! So you have to be careful. The tiniest variation in the formation of a letter can change the nuance of the meaning in subtle ways. So although the general trends will be there, you should tread lightly. One slip in interpretation could turn what is in fact a meek, well-mannered individual into a monster.

The best advice I can offer you is this: Never take one letter on its own and treat it as a rounded description of the person's character; use many different letters, put them together and build up your picture of the writer's personality from there.

In all cases, please be kind and generous in your appraisal. Give everyone a chance. It's too easy to criticize and pull people apart thread by tiny thread. You may have the power to do it, but that doesn't mean you should. Allow your subjects the benefit of the doubt whenever you can. Use your judgment. If you're going on a date, and in your view the handwriting paints a rosy picture of your partner but your intuition is screaming, "Danger—red alert!" then do yourself a favor: Heed the warning of your intuition and keep away. In the end, handwriting analysis only goes so far. It's down to the individual to judge what is right for him or her.

"There are so many variations on each letter, aren't there? Some of them I don't even recognize—why is that?"

Every country has its own preferred style of writing, one that reflects the specific outlook, attitudes and behavioral characteristics of its people. In the United

States, for instance, children are taught to write in a style that is strong, go-getting and full of glowing expectation for the future. American handwriting overflows with individuality and aspiration. Whereas in Great Britain the style has a much calmer look to it. It's less excitable, less expressive and generally reflects the overall image of the nation: the stiff upper lip, the self-control, the fear of revealing too much emotion. This book contains variations from many different countries. Those you don't recognize you can bet somebody else will.

"Most people tend to join up their letters when they write, don't they? But I don't. And I have a friend who only uses block capitals. Is that bad?"

No, it doesn't matter. Not really. Usually, handwriting that isn't "joined up" tends to belong to someone who is quite intense and plodding in their approach and has yet to find a way to relax and let go of their pent-up emotional energies.

    Someone who prints block letters rather than writes believes they're doing it to make their words more legible, but in reality they are merely attempting to disguise their true personality behind a kind of fake strength. Underneath they feel less comfortable and confident than they appear. Those capitals are their way of putting on a brave face for the rest of the world. But neither of these two styles is necessarily "bad." There is no such thing as totally bad handwriting anyway, just as there is no such thing as a totally bad person. Everything and everyone has something good to offer if we'll only take the time to look for it; I really believe that.

"What does it mean when the letters at the start of each word are very large and the rest of the letters in the word are small?"

This happens a lot. Usually it indicates a strong, flamboyant outer personality hiding a quieter, more serious and possibly analytical persona inside.

"And when the handwriting is a mixture of sizes—bIg aNd sMAll?"

This happens a lot, too. Assuming the writer has learned to write properly and there isn't some kind of mental or physical impairment interfering with the writing, then I always take it to mean that the person is struggling to grow up. He's trapped in an emotional no-man's-land, where the impulses he had when he was a teenager are battling it out against the urges he now feels as a fully grown adult (and this can apply at any age). Inside, there is pressure and confusion, both of which are very slowly being sorted out as maturity sets in.

"I have heard it said that if you change your writing it will change your life. Is it true that, since the way you write reflects the person

you are, then by changing your handwriting significantly overnight, you become a different person?"

I really don't believe any of this at all, I'm afraid.

You hear the "change your handwriting, change your life" proposal quite a lot in this business, and there are even one or two books about it, but it simply doesn't make sense to me. Think about it. Your handwriting is a physical manifestation of the inner you, reflecting all your most vital energies: emotional, sexual, spiritual, intellectual, physical and metaphysical. That energy works from the inside out. So if some fundamental part of you changes in some way—your beliefs, attitudes, values or whatever else—then the change will trickle through immediately into your handwriting. It's got to, that's logical. What's illogical is that it could somehow work the other way around.

Example: Suppose one day, out of the blue, you suddenly took a dislike to the shape of your v, having discovered to your horror that v's reveal to the whole world the size of your sexual appetite and your approach to the subject of sex generally. You loathe that v of yours, it's so cramped up and scrawly. From now on, you decide, you're going to do better: Every time you draw the letter v you'll make it bigger and wider and more inviting. The question is: Will your efforts have a knock-on effect on the power of your sex drive? Answer: Of course not! You can't make yourself perform better in bed simply by making your v's wider, although I confess it would be a wonderful world if you could. No, the changes first have to take place inside of you; that's where it really counts. If you were to expand your mind in relation to sex, to learn new techniques, experiment with different partners, explore the broader horizons of what is possible and enjoyable to you, then that will make a significant impact in the long term. The experience you gain, coupled with your refreshing change of attitude, must add vitality to your v, causing it to widen naturally as a result. As I said, it works from the inside out.

Deliberately changing your handwriting can no more change your life, in my view, than if you wear red socks instead of blue ones or decide to order crab cakes for lunch today instead of prawns.

"Okay, then, so what about the people who've made a study of fancy lettering and who practice it until their handwriting looks really ornate and beautiful?"

I know what you're saying. We call that italicized or calligraphic handwriting, the type you see printed on certificates or other formal documents. You're right—it can look beautiful, and there's nothing wrong with that at all.

The only time it means anything specific to us, though, is when a person adopts this style as a deliberate cover-up to prevent the rest of the world from seeing what his or her real writing looks like. In that kind of situation I see cal-

ligraphic script as a potential danger sign. It's telling me that the writer feels so insecure about the person he is that he's prepared to put on an exaggerated display on the outside in the hope that people will prefer the fake persona to the real one. To me, what it says is, "I really don't like myself very much, and you probably won't like me either; so, just in case, here's something beautiful to look at while I sneak away into a corner and hide."

Okay, maybe it's not as dramatic as that, but in the cases I've come across, it's not been far from the truth. In short, there are profound self-esteem issues waiting to be worked out here. The calligraphic writer needs to value himself more and gain a better insight into what he, as an individual, is offering the world. Nobody likes a fraud; we all want to feel we're dealing with the genuine article, so why deny the existence of something so precious—your real self—by covering it over with a false one? Every time I see someone struggling against the odds to be something he's not, I'm reminded of the wise words of Anwar al-Sadat: "Most people seek after what they do not possess and are thus enslaved by the very things they want to acquire." This can apply to personality and image just as much as it can to a new car or a big expensive house.

It's the stuff they write corny songs about, I know, but every single one of us is beautiful and perfect just as we are. There is no one exactly like you or me anywhere else in the world, no one with the same special qualities and gifts or the exact same purpose in life. We are unique. If our friends, our acquaintances or our critics don't happen to appreciate that fact and can't like us exactly the way we are, then maybe we ought to start associating with the kind of people who will. We shouldn't have to alter a single fragment of our personality, even in the smallest way, just to please others. Changes we make must be for our own benefit—otherwise why bother?

If this book has an underlying theme, I guess that's it. Be yourself. And if you haven't discovered who "yourself" is yet, then get started. And good luck!

Be content, submit to what is. Find happiness in freedom from desire.
If there is nothing you want, then you have everything.
If you have everything, you will be happy.
—Henry Knight Miller, *Life Triumphant*
